# STREAMED TO KILL

# EMMY ELLIS

# CHAPTER ONE

*E*very so often you come across a complete and
utter wanker.

David was with one now, some fucked-up bloke
he'd met ages ago while eating in here—the café
part of Morrisons—who sneered at him as though
he was a piece of shit. Yeah, one of *those* people,

someone who needed his head caved in and a few fingers removed.

David stifled a laugh at that and stared at the man. He didn't look like he belonged in here, suited up the way he was. David reckoned Conrad would fit better in a restaurant environment, where waiters hovered to do your bidding, hoping to be of such great service you gave them a hefty tip.

People, they got on David's nerves. Greedy for the most part, always wanting more.

A pinch of unease griped at his gut, and he sulkily acknowledged he was just as bad. He wanted more. To climb the ladder of success, only it wasn't a career ladder he had in mind. He wanted a personal journey, one where he tested how far he was prepared to go in order to sate the urges inside him. He wanted to be clever like Conrad was. He needed people to know *how* clever he was, so he could go around with a nice feeling in his belly that told him he'd been born male for a reason, that his shitty life up to now hadn't been a waste of time.

Conrad here, well, he was on the road to being a winner where he worked. He'd said, on numerous occasions—David zoning out half the time because Conrad was a boring bastard—that his boss had him earmarked for promotion. Conrad had been spinning that yarn for about four months now, and he was still in an office with several others, striving to get noticed.

*Reckon if he poked his tongue out it'd be brown he's licked so many arses.*

David knew all about wanting promotion. In his job, he'd been overlooked too many times to mention.

"So you see," Conrad said, pinching his chin as though deep in thought, when in reality he probably had his answer ready and waiting, knew exactly what he was going to say several sentences before he said it. "You have to give it to her. She knows how to dress."

They were going down that road again then, Conrad harping on about that woman. When would they have a conversation that *wasn't* about some bird Conrad fancied? David had to admit that yeah, the current woman in question knew how to dress. But he wasn't after her in *that* way—he'd fancied getting to know her for another reason entirely—but she obviously thought he'd just wanted to get into her knickers. She had to pay for that, assuming such a thing about him, but now wasn't the time. Not when he sat there, a pot of tea between him and Conrad and the remnants of a cooked breakfast on their plates.

"Been working here for ages, she has." Conrad eyed the woman, winking at her as if she'd be interested in a prick like him. A long lock of his black fringe bobbed. "Said this is her second job or something. Like, she has two. I reckon she'd be a right goer, don't you?"

David nodded—best thing to do with Conrad, otherwise, David would say something he might regret. Or, rather, *do* something. Not that he'd regret it as such, just... Yeah, well, this wasn't the time for thinking about what he'd like to do to Conrad either. Wouldn't sit right with some people if he picked up a knife and jabbed it into the man's eye, would it? Not when there hadn't been any provocation. Not when David just felt like doing it for fun, to see Conrad's reaction.

"I'm going to ask her out." Conrad scraped his chair back.

"Good luck with that." Anger sparked inside David. He had to leave before he picked up that knife. "Anyway, I gotta go." He stood and, walking away without looking back, left the shop.

Conrad might question him next time they ate together, asking what his problem had been, fucking off like that. But that was a conversation for another day, and besides, with Conrad so engrossed in his plans to snare that female, get her to go out on a date with him, he might not even have registered that David had gone.

The air outside hit him. Harder than that bitch the other month, the one who hadn't wanted him to—

He shoved those thoughts away and headed for his car, a beat-up Fiat the colour of shite. If he had a woman at home, the slapper would need feeding around now, but he *didn't* have anyone there, and the voice hadn't told him to make a move on the Morrisons girl yet. He was still angry about Conrad going to ask her out. If that bird in there got involved with him, it would fuck David's plans

4

up—ones he'd been making for the past couple of days.

*Jesus. Yeah, every so often you come across a complete and utter wanker.*

He didn't go to his car in the end. It always helped him to think, strolling did, so he took the path beside the supermarket then crossed the road, entering a dog-walking area where he'd met many women in the past. It appeared as just a massive field, but at the back was a dense forest where mutts liked to ignore their owners and go inside to investigate. It was always handy if the animals did that. When David wanted to chat a woman up—or let them think that was what he was doing—he parked on a rarely used road behind the trees, and whether they were willing to go with him or not, he bundled them into his car and took them home.

With the Morrisons café woman, he'd entertained many a scenario. He'd overheard her telling another customer she lived close, and that after her evening shift in the café she walked her hound here—had to do it as soon as she got home from work, seven-thirty on the dot, otherwise he'd piss in the hallway, happened every time. If only she knew how her seemingly innocent conversation had saved him the hassle of finding this shit out.

He strolled towards the trees, remembering how he'd met the other bitches here. The latest bitch...it had been a choice between two—one small and slim, the other tall and athletic-looking.

Small and slim won. Easier to manhandle if she had a mind to get away from him.

She hadn't, had fallen for his patter, hadn't she, all wide eyes and pink cheeks from a blush of embarrassment. He'd told her she was stunning— the lie had tripped easily off his tongue—and she'd agreed to get into his car, dog an' all, and go home with him. He'd plied her with tea, offered her some biscuits—'*God, no, you don't need to watch your weight, you're beautiful as you are. Go on, have a biccy!*'—and she'd relaxed.

Silly cow.

Her dog had proved a bind, though. The little bastard had wanted to go out, hadn't he, breaking the spell he'd cast over the woman, getting her anxious that he'd mess in David's flat.

"Let me do the honours," he'd said. "I can take him down to the patch of grass out the front and he can do his business there."

She'd agreed, but the dog hadn't managed to do his business. In the lift on the way down, the Yorkshire Terrier had nipped David's hand while in his arms and, well, that had annoyed him.

He'd strangled the bloody thing, then returned to his flat, dog still in his arms, and put it beside the front door, as though it had died suddenly, all by itself. Later, the woman had got up to investigate and stood in the living room doorway, staring down at her pet, her mouth a perfect O.

He'd had to shut her up before she'd screamed.

### *Diary Entry #307*

*<u>Quote for the day: I am the fucking man!</u>*

*I heard that voice again this morning. The one that tells me to get the girls. 'Get the girls, get the girls, go out there and get the girls.' It's as though that voice was made just for me. And maybe it was. Maybe whoever it belongs to knows everything about me. Knows I'd follow his instructions. The first time I heard it— Shit myself, didn't I, but the more it spoke, the more I got used to it.*

*The more sense it made.*

*It's been with me for years.*

*That woman with the Yorkshire Terrier. She's long gone. It's funny, but it doesn't freak me out, the thought of getting rid of them. It ought to, me living in a flat where anyone could see me out of their windows. But I usually wait until about three in the morning when most are in bed—and those who aren't probably wouldn't be staring outside at an empty street anyway. On the nights I do a body dump, I carry them over my shoulder. Put them in the car boot, shut the lid on their dead-as-fuck faces.*

*Their eyes. They go like those old gits you see who are getting gyp from their cataracts going dodgy on them. Grey clouds over blue moons. And they're always blue. I'm not into brown-eyed birds.*

*They're useless to me in the end, those women. All of them have been. None of them have liked what I do. I just need to keep going until I find the one who does. And they've been missed by people. I like that.*

*Them being missed, no fucker knowing where they are, everyone frantic as to where they've gone. The newspaper reports—Jesus, anyone would think I'd done something wrong. But how can my personal journey be wrong?*

*It's time to sort out the Morrisons girl. Feed her a bit, give her some water. She's started to get on my nerves, which is a shame. There's only so long I can keep them before I get bored of waiting for The Time. The initial rush wears off, and that's something the voice didn't warn me about, but I'll learn to deal with it.*

*But she's drifting off to sleep when she shouldn't, not at night the same as normal people, and sometimes I can't wake her. I've had to splash her face with water, because kicking her in the kidney didn't work.*

*The needle seems to be stronger with this one.*

*She's the one from the supermarket. It didn't take much to lure her here. Recognised me, didn't she, and she thought I gave a flying fuck about her dog. That mutt gave me pause, though. Big bastard. I was prepared to take it with us an' all. The voice wouldn't let me, though. Said it was better off out of the way, one less body to dump, one less thing to deal with when The Time came.*

*I wonder how long I'll get to keep this woman?*

*Tally:*

*#1. Bird with the scraggly black hair and the yappy dog. Joanne. Came home with me last year.*

8

*Remained a day or two until she outstayed her welcome. I couldn't handle her whining. She ended up in the stream down behind the dog-walking field. Discovered in March. Small news, just this little section at the bottom of the first page, like she didn't deserve a big mention. She didn't, but I did.*

*#2. Slag. Smelt funny. No dog, just happened to be taking a shortcut. Good for me, crap for her. She stayed about a week, that one, because she did as she was told and didn't give me any hassle when I stroked her cheek, unless you count wincing as hassle. That was in June. Her name was Lorraine. Bit of a bigger mention in the local paper, but not what I was after. Not what the voice wanted. A long slim column right down the side of the front page. Murmurings of the bodies being connected because she was found in the same stream.*

*#3. Married this time—had been for three years, she'd said. Faithful. Loved her fella. They'd wanted kids, were trying for one. Deborah. Or, at first—'Oh, hi, nice to meet you. Call me Debbie or Deb, everyone else does!'*

*When was she? November. It was cold again, I know that.*

*Much bigger coverage with her. She was the first bitch to get front-page news in the bottom half of the nationals, not just the local. A proud moment, that one. Stream dump again. Discovered in late December. And you'd think they'd have kept a better eye out down there, wouldn't you? Saying that, the spaces in time between them being put there were kind of random—good idea from the voice—and no police force has the manpower to set a copper up down there twenty-four seven, every day of the year.*

*If they did, my personal journey would be interrupted.*

*#4. Brown hair—short, unusual for me—and she did my head in from day one. Should have gone with my gut in not inviting her home, but the voice had insisted. Now, she was around the July mark—July of this year. Bit of a gap, what with Christmas barging in and me getting that new job that fucked up when I could do my thing. Emma. Bad girl, always complaining, saying her parents would be worrying. So?*

*Excellent coverage, made the nationals again.*

*#5. That bloody cow with the Yorkshire Terrier. Maria. Irritating. Noisy. Didn't stay long. I can't even bear to write about her. The worst one yet.*

*#6. Cheryl. Current. Now here's another funny thing. That Langham, the detective on the case, he works with this fella, who also works for the local newspaper. You following me? Well, Cheryl only bloody works at the paper, too. Receptionist, she said, doing a second job in the café at Morrisons, mornings and evenings. Oh my God. That is such a classic.*

*More on her as things progress. I have to go. She's banging on the wall for a bit of attention.*

# CHAPTER TWO

Langham stared around the incident room. It needed painting. The pea-soup-green walls were peeling, and scuff marks had them looking shabby. A couple of posters—men wanted from God knew how long ago—had curling corners, the faces of the criminals going cream in places where they'd been on show since before the no-smokingin-the-workplace law. Nicotine, it got everywhere. Like the scum of society. The bastards who kept him in a job.

The officers on shift stared back at him, expressions ranging from bored to weary to blank. All they had to deal with at the moment were ongoing cases, small shit that shouldn't take long to wrap up but did, or the case involving the missing women that had gone stone cold. If he were honest, it had never even come close to being hot.

The people sitting before him seemed like they could do with an honest-to-goodness massive case to get their teeth into. He knew how they felt. It wasn't that they waited for murder, longed for it, but when one cropped up, everyone went into a different zone.

More alert. More focused. More on the sodding ball.

He'd saved the missing women's case discussion until last. It was the biggest on their list, but they weren't getting anywhere with it. Women disappeared, were found in the stream, and nothing he or his team had done had come up with anything to help them find the killer. No evidence of where they'd been prior to being murdered and dumped—except the snippet Oliver had been given from one of them while she'd still been alive. Other than that? Sweet fuck all.

Langham turned from his officers and dragged across the largest whiteboard on wheels, which had several victims' pictures pinned on it along with their information scrawled in marker underneath. He thought about what had happened that day a while ago—him and Oliver eating lunch in Langham's office and some woman speaking to Oliver in his head. How the fuck Oliver dealt with that went beyond anything Langham could imagine. Dead people speaking to you all your life, then suddenly people who were alive? He couldn't fathom it, could find no rational explanation either, just that it happened and had provided crucial information on previous cases.

He wished it would provide crucial information now. Before some other poor bitch got offed.

Langham sighed and faced the group again. Some of them had perked up a bit—a few pictures of dead, water-bloated bodies could do that to a copper—but the rest appeared as though they wanted to get up and go home. He didn't blame them. *He* wanted to go home, and they'd only been here an hour.

"Yeah, yeah," he said, holding up a hand as if that might stop anyone walking the hell out. "We've been through this before, I know. But it's Friday, recon time—same thing every week—and something we just have to get on with. Now, I'll be honest with you, this case is pissing me off. As you know, we have no new leads—none whatsoever. So we're dealing with a man—yes, or a woman, but highly unlikely, given the profile—who is meticulous. This is planned, all of it, right down to the last detail. Nothing is left to chance, like he has every avenue covered. With a bloke like that, we

15

need to watch out. He'll get worse. Now, because he's killed more than three women, we all know that levitates him to serial status. Not good for us, but good for him. He'll be feeling the power, might slip up. So, what else can we do here? Suggestions?"

Detective Wickes held up one hand then lowered it to cross both arms over his chest and tuck his fingers beneath his armpits. His brown hair needed a good cut but, like Langham, he probably couldn't find the time. "We could up the patrol at the stream. I said that from the start."

Langham sniffed. "Yes, we could, but that stream is long, and as you know, the killer hasn't established a secure pattern. The time between the women going missing is getting shorter—he's getting braver, needs the thrill sooner, he needs less time to recover or go over the previous kill as a means of gaining satisfaction. We could send men out every evening to check, but only certain points of the stream can be covered at any one time. While our men are patrolling the north end, he could be dumping a body at the other."

Wickes sighed. He knew the drill. The excuses.

"So," Langham went on, "as much as I'd like to put officers at strategic points along that stream every night until our killer gets spotted either abducting or dumping his victims, I can't. It all boils down to costs, too, you know that. While, say, four to six officers are at the stream, others are stretched to breaking point out on the streets. Cut me some slack on that. I can't make it happen."

Wickes pinched his chin between finger and thumb. "It's a pisser, though. We just have to sit and wait for another body to show up. Fucking stinks."

"It does," Langham agreed, "but there is the other alternative. When a woman goes missing, we start acting right away. No more 'let's see if she returns after forty-eight hours' crap. We look into it immediately. Granted, a lot of manpower will go into that, but it's all we can do, and it's easier to manage that into our schedules. A quick phone call here and there chasing up the women's last whereabouts isn't the same as taking a chunk of time using several officers to man the stream."

He held back a sigh and went on. "As we know from experience—and I wish we didn't—most of the women will turn up again—just some worried husband or mother calling in because she's half an hour late—but at some point there'll be those who *don't* come home when it gets dark. Those are the red flags."

Sergeant Villier raised her hand then lowered it to her lap. A leggy blonde, thirtysomething, she looked weird in uniform. It didn't suit her. She seemed the type who'd be more at home in a basque and stockings. Anyone who had the guts to suggest such a thing would soon find she didn't agree. She'd rip the balls off a man who came on to her at work—or anywhere else, Langham suspected.

"Yes, Villier?" he held his breath for her comment.

She was likely to go into one, shoving her opinion out there with such force that when he had to gently shoot down her ideas it would make everyone feel uncomfortable. She meant well, but shit, she was a pushy one.

"I think we've gone as far as we can go here." She stood and joined Langham up front.

He bit back the urge to tell her to sit the fuck back down. She had a habit of doing this kind of thing, encroaching on his position, trying to get the others to see that her standing as the uniformed officers' boss was just one step of her ladder. She intended to climb higher, that much was obvious.

Villier faced the others. "Let's go through what we have."

*I was just about to do that after the question-and-answer session. Christ.*

She continued, strutting back and forth, her black trousers rustling with each step. "We know he abducts them from the field opposite Morrisons supermarket. As Langham said, having our men at the stream each night isn't going to work. The same goes for having them either at the abduction field, the forest behind it, or inside the supermarket. The killer will know by now that he'll possibly be spotted. He has to take more care—and he will. I'm going to propose something and, while I know none of you would want this, and I appreciate your concern, I really do, I can't sit idly by and wait for another woman's body to turn up. I joined the force because..."

*Fuck. Here we go...*

Langham half-listened to how she wanted to rid the city of criminals, and while she couldn't do that by herself, she'd give it a damn good try. Her father had been a copper, her grandfather before that, blah-de-fucking-blah. About to step in and stop her diatribe, he was brought up short by her strident voice cutting into his thoughts.

"...as bait." She slammed her hands onto her hips and eyed everyone, then her gaze finally fell on Langham.

"What?" He hadn't expected that. Yes, she was dedicated—more dedicated than most of the people there—but to offer herself up like that? No fucking way. It hadn't come to that. Not yet.

"I'll be one of the women," she said. "A dog walker. I'll go every evening at the same time. Walk the field's perimeter and see if I spot anyone suspicious. I mean, we should have done this ages ago. I did say, but no one listened." She huffed out a breath. "Or they listened but didn't agree to it."

She was getting at him—he'd obviously tuned her out when she'd suggested it before—but his hands were tied anyway from those above him. Sending her out there wouldn't just be sending her out. Other officers would have to be involved, watching her as she walked, and sparing so many men *every* night... They had no solid idea of when the next victim was likely to be abducted, so her idea just wasn't viable.

He explained that to her.

She narrowed her eyes. "Just as I thought. Silly of me to suggest such a thing."

Langham smiled, going for a genuine one but thinking he'd missed it by a bloody long shot. "Besides, you're blonde."

She frowned, shaking her head as though he was the thickest fucker she'd seen in a long time.

"He hasn't taken a blonde." Langham gestured to the pictures on the board. "All brunettes, all blue-eyed. A brown-eyed blonde wouldn't pique his interest."

Villier's cheeks flushed. She'd never admit to not seeing that obvious fact—or having not been listening when he'd pointed it out a few weeks ago.

She sighed. "Um, hello? Wigs? Contact lenses? Heard of them?"

Her tone and attitude got on his last nerve. Sod going gently on her now. "While I appreciate your input, in future you're better off giving it from your seat, like everyone else does. Also, as the *leading detective inspector* on this case, I get to decide whether we take such a drastic step. As for hearing about wigs and contact lenses? Yes, I tend to wear them on the nights I go out, I thought you knew that."

Rumbles of laughter. A whoop.

"Now, *Sergeant* Villier, please return to your seat, and I'll write your suggestion on the board. We *may* discuss it at a later date, but at the moment it's a no-go."

She stared at him, cheeks getting redder, then turned away and made a dignified walk back to her chair. He'd been a bastard to her, showing her up like that in front of everyone, but she'd pushed his buttons, and his reprimand had been a long time coming. He didn't want to tell his boss about her, but if she continued like this, he'd have to.

He changed the subject. "The newspapers. While we can't control everything that gets printed, we can minimise the damage. So far, the local papers have done as we've asked and kept the articles on the women low profile. Unfortunately, a couple of nationals picked up on it, but they haven't sensationalised it as they usually would. Thankfully, it seems no one from the big guys has joined the dots just yet and realised these cases are linked." He sighed. "But, as we all know, it won't be long, and this will be because the killer will be hacked off that he isn't making full-frontal, national news. Yes, he's made the front page, but with an ego the size of a house, he's going to want more. And that means he'll up his game. Do something more shocking."

"What can be more shocking than what he's already done?" a male uniform asked. "I mean, he's abducting and killing women, for Christ's sake."

"Ah," Langham said. "Hastings, isn't it?"

The officer nodded.

"New, aren't you?" Langham said. "You haven't seen anything yet. What this man is doing is terrible, yes, but so far, the bodies have only been wrecked by the stream itself. Imagine if they'd been wrecked by him as well." He pressed on, wanting to put his meaning across so this wet-behind-the-ears kid would get the bloody drift pretty quick. "What if he stabbed them? Sliced their skin to ribbons so when we found them they didn't look like women at all? What if you had to go to a scene and stand there staring down at such a sight, holding back puke as it threatened to come up and contaminate the scene? What if he carved into their faces, gouged out their eyes? You getting the picture here, son?"

Hastings' face was pale, the tips of his ears red.

"Good. So, back to the newspapers. What I've described to Hastings may well start happening. Who knows what goes on in a killer's head. Something might tip him over the edge so he deviates from what is the norm to him, which is drugging them into unconsciousness and placing them face-first in the stream and watching them drown in their sleep. There *has* to be a reason he does this, and sadly, it won't become clear until he's caught and he chooses to tell us. Which he will if he's the type we think he is and wants attention. I'll need whoever has the newspapers on their list to telephone them again and make sure any future stories remain small."

"Won't that encourage him to go out of control?" Wickes asked.

"It's possible, but the least amount of panic generated for the local women the better. And yes, I'm well aware not making a big fuss potentially puts women in more danger, but I'm following orders myself and passing them down to you."

Langham gave Villier a direct glare then shifted his gaze to check he hadn't frightened the life out of Hastings. The kid—must be twenty if he was a day—chewed the inside of his lip and bounced one foot on the floor. He appeared as though he needed to get out, get some fresh air. Langham knew all about *that.*

"Right. Those reviewing the morgue files, review them again. Those going through the witness statements, go through them again. Those doing whatever you're doing on this case, go through it again. I want this fucker caught. Sooner rather than later, got it?"

# CHAPTER THREE

David gained perverse pleasure in sitting with Conrad, knowing where the Morrisons woman was when Conrad didn't. Of course, David sat there making all the right noises, offering all the right reasons why she might not be serving them this morning, but Conrad was more upset than David had thought he'd be. What David *hadn't*

bargained for was the bloke really did like Cheryl, wanted her for more than a bit of fun in the sack. He seemed overly upset by her absence.

How had David missed that? Had he been so intent on snaring her for his own reasons that he hadn't fully realised how much Conrad wanted to secure a date with her? Then again, David had walked out of the café last time, hadn't he, pissed off and seeing red, and when Conrad had been speaking to him prior to that, he hadn't particularly been listening. Oh, he'd heard him, but he hadn't taken it all in *properly*. He needed to watch himself for that kind of thing in the future. He could miss important info that might change the course of his operation.

"She told me she'd meet me, David, go on a date with me. Can you believe that?"

David took a deep breath. Plonked on a fake smile. "Wow, how cool is that?"

"Not very. She didn't turn up. At first, I reckoned it was because I'd forgotten to give her my number, but I thought back and *know* she took it. I'd written it on a napkin, remember doing it." He shoved a hand through his bugging, bouncy fringe. "Then I thought she'd tossed it away, didn't have any intention of meeting me at all, especially when I called her and her phone went straight to voicemail. But now she isn't here either... Something isn't right, is it?"

"No idea," David said. "Last time I heard anything, you were going to ask her out. I haven't been here since to know how long she's been gone." He wanted to laugh. Really laugh.

"It's been two days, mate. Two bloody days. And where were you yesterday anyway? I waited here for you, but you didn't bloody show." Conrad stabbed at a sausage.

David decided it might be a good idea to ignore Conrad's questions. "Oh, well, she might just be ill then. Two days is nothing. It isn't unheard of, you know. People get sick, switch off their phones. Christ, you ought to calm down." David rammed a bacon rasher into his mouth and chewed, enjoying what he privately called the 'piggy' flavour.

"David, I asked her coworker. That old dear over there who always gives us lukewarm tea. Cheryl didn't call in sick. No one here has heard from her." Conrad sighed, glancing around the café as though Cheryl would appear at any moment, out of breath, late for her shift, full of apologies that she hadn't met him.

"I'd say she might have switched shifts—you know she only works early mornings and late afternoons here, doing a stint at the newspaper in between, you told me earlier you'd found that out—but if she hasn't called in..." David shrugged. "Maybe she just got pissed off with working two jobs. Who fucking knows?"

Conrad sat up straighter. "The newspaper. You reckon I should go there, check if they've seen her?"

David frowned, rolling his eyes as though he thought Conrad was going too far. "Oh, come on!

27

Don't you think that would look a bit weird? A bit stalkerish?"

Now he thought about it, Conrad going to the newspaper might be just the thing David needed. Conrad turning up, saying he was meant to have been meeting her, and him ringing her as often as he had, might raise red flags. The editor might take him for one of those nutters who involved themselves with their crimes, trying to help solve it when all along they were diverting the police elsewhere.

"On second thought," David said, "you go to the newspaper. Great idea. Go and check, and if she isn't there or hasn't been since you last saw her, then I'd say there was something to worry about. Maybe they're shrugging her absence off like this lot are—that she just didn't turn up. Maybe no one knows she's actually missing." David stressed that last word and waited for Conrad to freak the fuck out.

Conrad paled. His hand holding his fork shook, and the sausage wiggled along with it. "Oh my God. What if she's one of those women?"

David scooped up some baked beans. "What women?" He knew full well what bloody women, he just wanted Conrad to talk about them. About him. He put the beans in his mouth and swallowed without chewing. Pointless chewing beans.

"You know, the ones found in the river. What if that weirdo took her?" Two spots of pink appeared on Conrad's cheekbones. His mouth quivered.

*Jesus H, he's gone and got himself well and truly attached to her.*

"I doubt it. Wasn't she ultra-careful? I remember her saying to a customer once that she had a big dog, never went out alone without it. No way would someone be able to take her without being bitten." *Liar. That dog was soft as shit, and the knife went into his belly nice and easy.*

Conrad pointed his still-sausage-laden fork in David's direction. "Good point. I'm just being silly, aren't I?"

*Most definitely not, tosser.* "Maybe a bit. But I understand where you're coming from. Just didn't realise you liked her enough to be bothered if she never met you for a date, that's all."

"What? Don't piss about! I talked about her *all* the time. I thought you knew."

David shook his head. "Um, no, wasn't that obvious to me, but then again, I can be a bit slow on the uptake." Best to let him think he was dim, that he wouldn't have the nous to be That Weirdo.

David was tempted to do just what he hoped Conrad would actually do—involve himself with Cheryl's disappearance, find out what was going on from the other side—but quickly decided against it. He preferred guessing what Langham would do next—if anything—and congratulating himself when he'd guessed right, had predicted the detective's moves. This time, though, he was treading on rockier ground. Yeah, the others had been missed by loved ones, but this one, well, Langham's psychic aide knew Cheryl, and they

29

would possibly push that little bit harder to find her. David had done his research before taking her. The thing was, Cheryl wasn't so bad, nice company when she wasn't sleeping, and he wouldn't mind keeping her for longer. That might be dangerous, though. They could discover where she was, then it would be game over, his personal journey cut off before it had even properly begun.

Conrad sipped his tea from a white cup, the kind found in most cafés that held the equivalent of half a cup of a normal brew. Two or three gulps, and the bloody stuff was gone, which was why they always shared a pot. David reached out to pour himself a fresh one, surreptitiously watching Conrad as he stared out of the window at the numerous rows of parked cars. David would feel sorry for him if he could be bothered, but Conrad was such a bore, such a wanker, that he couldn't muster up the energy. He'd enjoy being the one Conrad turned to when Cheryl was found. The man would be cut up, he'd bet, snivelling into his cooked breakfast or his lukewarm tea.

Why didn't they provide tea cosies here? Another thing to add to his irritation list. Maybe he'd ask Cheryl when he got home.

***Diary entry #308***

*Quote of the day: The man who can successfully hide a multitude of emotions, making others think he feels the complete opposite, is a clever man indeed. I am clever.*

*In the car on the way back from Morrisons, I got to thinking about Conrad going to the newspaper. What a cock! If they don't take him seriously, that's fine by me—I want to play with that detective for a long while to come—but if they do, I might need to be a bit more careful. The voice told me not to worry, that there's nothing to fret about, but you can never be sure, can you?*

*I asked what the voice's name was as I drove along Hipwell Road, and he replied that if I needed a name, Mr Clever would do. I wanted to laugh, to tell him he was just as much a dick as Conrad, but sensed that wasn't a wise move. Mr Clever gets prickly sometimes, snaps at me when I won't do what he wants, when he wants, and as I'm at a crucial part of the bitch's place in my personal journey, I can't be doing with anything going wrong. If Mr Clever decided to stop instructing me, letting me know when it's safe and when it isn't, I'd be fucked, wouldn't I?*

*I must admit, his advice in telling me to wear a disguise when I took Cheryl was genius. He said I must do that with every woman in the future. That detective's aide might have the means to speak to her and get my description. The newspaper said that Oliver bloke not only hears the voices of the dead but now has the ability to speak to people who are alive—using his mind. How insane is that? I don't believe a sodding word of it, but there you go.*

31

*So when I got back to my flat, I had to come in here and get the disguise out of my bedside drawer. It's just a mask. You know, the one I got from eBay yonks ago, that supplier from Hong Kong. I remember the package took ages to arrive, and back then I'd wondered if I'd have it in time for that Halloween party the knobs down in flat sixty-two were holding. I think, if I recall right, that's detailed in Diary Entry #168.*

*I thought I'd quickly scribble a few words down before going in to see her. She was being noisy when she heard me arrive home, so I now I have to teach her a lesson with the needle.*

*Back in a minute...*

*I taught her that lesson all right. That calling out doesn't get you anywhere.*

*She's gone quiet now. Good girl.*

David opened the bedroom door and peered around it. Cheryl was where he'd left her, on the mattress. She'd messed the sheets instead of getting up to use the baby's potty in the corner. That wasn't very nice. He'd have to clean them now.

Or maybe he ought to make her do it. Perhaps she wouldn't shit the bed again then.

"Get up," he said, his words muffled behind the latex. Sweat beaded above his upper lip, and he got a shiver of pleasure down his back from it.

She lifted the top half of her body and stared at him, seemingly uncomprehending. Was she thick?

He didn't think she should be, being a newspaper secretary. She ought to know a thing or two, know her onions, as people were fond of saying.

An annoying phrase, that.

"I said, get up!"

He sounded menacing, and it gave him a thrill to watch her scrabbling to her feet, unsteady where she'd been sleeping on and off. That medicine he got from the bloke down The Stick was brilliant. Made a person off their face. It was wearing off now, what with her calling out the way she had, and she was due another dose. But first she needed to clean that bedding.

"Now pick up those sheets and come with me. Make sure you fold them around your mess. I don't want any of it dropping on my floors."

He left the room, waiting for her in the hallway. It struck him that if she'd shit the bed she'd also crapped in her clothes. He had nothing here for her except what the other girls used to wear. Those would have to do, or she could go naked. Whatever.

She came to stand beside him, and he turned his nose up. She didn't smell too wonderful.

"You need to have a bath. You can put the sheets in there with you. They'll need bleaching, and so do you. Bleach is such a fine cleaner, you know. It'll scour any impurities from your skin. Might burn a bit, but if it burns then you know it's working. The bathroom is this door here." He walked to it and pointed. "You have ten minutes. I'll be standing outside. It's pointless to check whether you can escape from the window because we're several floors up. Plus"—he'd said that last word in a growl—"I've locked it, so again, pointless. Just have your bath, and I'll come and get you when your time is up. Three, two, one— Go!"

He flung the door open and pushed her inside. She staggered forward into the cistern, banging her hip on it. A corner of the sheet dangled in the toilet.

"Look at what you're doing, Cheryl," he said, nodding at the loo.

She glanced at it.

*He* glanced at his watch.

"Nine minutes left. Get on with it." He shut the door and stood in front of it, spreading his legs and folding his hands over his chest. He felt like a god, all powerful, and smiled, his cheeks bunching, the skin there touching the underside of the mask. It was slippery from condensation.

Nine minutes was a long time when you were waiting. It dragged by, and David almost went in there when she still had fifty-two seconds to go.

Mr Clever said, *"Don't you think it odd that there've been no splashing sounds?"*

David frowned.

*"Don't you worry that she has a sheet in there, one long enough to hang herself with?"*

David cleared his throat.

*"Don't you wonder whether she didn't run a bath at all and has stuffed that sheet down her throat in the hopes she suffocates herself?"*

34

David looked at his watch again. Time to go into the bathroom. Mr Clever had worried him, though. There *hadn't* been any sounds of water running. Had he zoned out again and just hadn't heard it? She *might* have killed herself. She might be behind the door, waiting for him to enter. He pondered on how he should deal with this.

He yanked down the door handle and stared at her on the floor beside the toilet, intending to give her more than a piece of his mind—the whole damn chunk of it was ready and waiting on the tip of his tongue, the words it held ready to spill.

Cheryl was asleep, her face pressed against the pedestal, the sheet clutched in both hands and drawn up in a bunch beneath her chin. The stench was evil, what with the bathroom being small and the window closed. He sighed, bent down to take the sheet away, to peel her disgusting clothes off and put them in the wash. The machine would do the business on a ninety-degree cycle, but he couldn't fit her in there, too.

Asleep or not, she needed that bleach bath.

# CHAPTER FOUR

Langham was in his office, going over the missing women's files. Eleven-fifty in the bloody morning, and he was flicking one page after the other, seeing nothing he hadn't seen before, nothing that would help him out. He was antsy, pissed off that they were dealing with someone so cunning. It wasn't the first time he'd dealt with men like this, not by a long shot, but by now, after so many women had been found, something usually stood out, helping them break the case.

He ran everything through his head, the gnawed end of a biro between his teeth. All right, the killer had stuck to the same methods so far, abducting, keeping them from two to six days, drugging then dumping. Why had he kept some longer than others? Langham scoured the dates to check whether a pattern cropped up, but he just couldn't see anything of importance there.

"Get a fucking grip." He stabbed at the desk blotter with the pen nib. "Think. Go through it." He took a sip of tea and grimaced. "No bloody good. Can't think with cold tea."

He left his office, walking down the hospital-like corridor past the vending machine, resisting the urge to buy a packet of crisps and a bar of chocolate. Maybe a can of Coke. At the end, he leant on the wall and stared into the main working area, satisfied the others were actually doing their jobs and not piss-arsing about. Heads were bent, fingers tapping on keyboards, hands lifting coffees to lips.

"They're dumped on weekdays," he murmured, pushing off the wall and going into the small kitchen. "So it looks like weekends mean something. Like he works them. Probably lives alone or is keeping them in another location other than his home." He filled the kettle and put it on to boil. There was coffee in the percolator, but it'd already be stewed by now, not something he fancied on an empty belly. That stuff had the ability to melt his stomach lining.

He propped his elbows on the worktop and held his forehead in his hands. Glared at breadcrumbs. The casing of a straw from one of those Ribena cartons. The empty packet of sugar—Starbucks, whose wages ran to bloody Starbucks?—a splatter of coffee marring one corner, drying the paper and the sugar inside into a crinkled clump.

The kettle snapped off, the riotous bubble of the water drawing him back to the reason he was in here. Billows of steam huffed out of the spout, and he lost himself in the inane act of making tea. He stared at the cup as he squeezed the teabag, seeing it but not, going through the motions but hardly aware he was doing them. It helped him to think, staring—something Oliver had got the wrong end of the stick about when they'd worked the Sugar Strands case.

Tea made, he returned to his office, pushing the door open then going inside, taking a sip at the same time. Hot. Lovely.

Oliver sat in Langham's chair, his feet propped up on the desk, as usual, files pushed aside like so much refuse—as usual.

"What the hell are you doing here?" Langham glanced at the wall clock. "Nothing interesting going on at the newspaper? No tea to make for the editor?" He walked over to him. "Shift your arse. Get your own seat."

Oliver rose then walked to the one opposite. He plopped down and gave Langham one of those looks—the kind that said he'd received information. Relieved but feeling guilty for it, Langham sat and leant back. Whether it was data for the missing women case or something entirely different, it didn't matter. So long as a case got solved with Oliver's help, that'd be all right with him.

"What have you got?" He studied Oliver's face for signs he'd seen something horrific.

"Cheryl Witherspoon." Oliver clamped his jaw, the muscles there undulating beneath the skin.

She clearly meant something to Oliver, what with that flickering tic on his cheek, but Langham had never heard of her. Not that he could remember anyway.

"Who?" Langham swivelled his seat and opened a desk drawer, pulled out a packet of biscuits, then put them on the desk, wincing—crumbs scuttled out and spread far and wide, one of them getting stuck in a groove in the wood next to a small outcrop of dust. "Want one?" He took one for himself, examining it for foreign matter, fluff and whatnot from the drawer.

"No, I don't." Oliver was pale. Eyes hooded. Jaw muscles still flickering.

Not good.

"She wasn't at work again today." Oliver shook his head. "I didn't think anything of it. She's pulled sickies before if she's tired from working two jobs."

"Aww, fuck." Langham sighed, the name glaring bright-pink neon in his head now. "Not Cheryl from your office?"

"Yep." Oliver scooted forward and rested his forearms on the desk.

Langham put his biscuit back down. "Dead or alive?"

Oliver stared at the crumbs. "Alive when she spoke to me. Now? Fuck knows. No contact for an hour. She was...she was having a bath."

Langham picked up the biscuit again, bit off a chunk, and chewed. At times like this, it was better to let Oliver get it all out. Difficult, though, for Langham to keep quiet, to not push for information. When people contacted Oliver while Langham was there, Christ, it was hard to keep his mouth shut and wait for Oliver to repeat what he'd been told.

Oliver blinked, attention still on the crumbs. He seemed lost elsewhere, seeing something other than those crumbs. "Being bathed."

A frisson of unease sneaked up Langham's spine. Something was off here. Being bathed meant—

"Bathed by that man," Oliver said.

Shit. He'd known they had a whacko on their hands, but Christ, if that killer was washing them...

Oliver cleared his throat. "The man who..."

*The man who's taking the women.*

"In bleach," Oliver said.

"What the fuck?" Langham blurted, dropping the last bite of biscuit. "Jesus fuck— Sorry. Sorry.

Go on." He resisted asking questions. *Where is she? What does he look like? When was she taken? How long ago was she taken? Has he treated her okay?* He almost laughed at that. Bathing her in bleach was a good indication the man wasn't right in the head.

"It stinks—of two things," Oliver said. "The bleach is strong—I'd say he uses the undiluted kind, you know, the thick stuff, and lots of it. Plus, she shit herself."

"I'm sure any woman would be frightened."

"No, she *literally* shit herself," Oliver said.

"Oh. Fuck."

"That's why she was in the bath. He took her from the Morrisons field—she can't remember when, said time has skewed—and killed her dog then forced her into his car. She can't recall what type, just that it's brown."

Things were making sense. He'd wondered where some of the dogs had gone from the previous cases. The man clearly liked the idea of getting rid of two bodies, one with skin, the other with fur. Did that have some significance? Did the woman *have* to have a dog with them in order for him to approach them? If that were true, that was something, at least. Women who didn't walk dogs were safe, but he couldn't totally rule out that they weren't until he had more information. Besides, he was wrong there. One of the earlier women hadn't owned one.

Before he could stop himself, Langham said, "What does he look like? Where did he take her?"

"She doesn't know. He drugged her. She wasn't with it for the whole journey, mainly spent it with her eyes closed. She'd tried to work out where he was taking her by judging the turns he took, but she spaced out and lost track. As for what he looks like... He wore a mask. One of those latex things. Dark peach with wrinkles all over it, except the cheeks are smooth. She remembered thinking that was weird. It's got holes, so she could see his eyes. Green."

"A mouth hole?" Langham sipped his tea, trying not to lean forward, invade Oliver's space, put pressure on him.

"Yeah, like a scream, like someone's screaming. Wonky." Oliver closed his eyes.

Langham held his breath, waiting for the images to fill Oliver's mind. That was a recent development, Oliver being able to see—or rather, know things. He'd said it was like an information dump, data swooping into his head so he just knew, as though someone had told him.

Oliver shuddered. "Shit, it isn't nice. The eyeholes sort of droop down, like one of those Hush Puppy dogs, and the mouth is the same, except it's a sideways version. He has pink lips, dark pink—no idea whether he wears lipstick or what—and blond stubble, like, a day or two's worth. Possibly from him being too lazy to shave, but I get the impression he prefers it like that. Makes him feel manly, less of a kid—and that's a key point. He doesn't want to feel like a kid."

43

This was good, a major breakthrough. But what did that mean? Were they dealing with a youth? It wasn't unheard of that teenagers or those just entering manhood killed, but to such a degree... Shit, was it someone who'd just gone out on a whim to murder before he'd nurtured his needs for years like other serials usually did? Or had he been having thoughts of killing like this since he'd been a lad?

"He's...young," Oliver said. "I get the sense he's no more than twenty-five."

"Jesus," Langham breathed.

To find out a serial killer was so adept at that age was frightening. If they never found him, if he continued on this path, the man would grow in confidence and his acts might become unparalleled by the time he hit forty. A force to be reckoned with.

A force Langham intended to stop before it got any stronger.

"So, like I said," Oliver went on, "he jabbed her with something sharp, and it made her woozy. Got to rewind a second... He injected her at the bloody dog field. She couldn't walk. He dragged her through the forest to his car—he parks it on the other side of the woods—and shoved her on the back seat. She wanted to call out but couldn't speak, like her mouth wasn't working properly. She couldn't get up, couldn't move."

Langham gritted his teeth. A sharp pain shot up into his head, so he relaxed his jaw. Took another sip of tea while jotting down notes. So this man had access to drugs, needles. Was he a doctor? Langham wrote down that he'd need to take a look at how long it took for someone to become a doctor, what the youngest age was. Or was he an assistant, some bloke who worked in a GP's office or hospital?

Oliver sniffed. "She wasn't sure how long they'd travelled, she lost track of where they might be going, and by the time they arrived at his place, she couldn't open her eyes. I get the feeling like they were glued shut, but they weren't. It was just the drug doing its thing. He got her out of the car, put her over his shoulder."

So he had no restrictions? He could just take people to his place without worrying someone might see? Did he live out in the countryside then? Somewhere like Dorton, a sleepy village where no one saw much after nine o'clock because they were sequestered behind their closed curtains, sitting on sofas, too engrossed in what was on TV for them to see anything else? Langham noted that down. So many bloody questions, the answers remaining elusive. Fuck, he needed more.

"And then?" Langham prompted quietly.

"She remembered the sound of his feet and the feeling of going upwards, up some stairs—lots of stairs."

*A flat. So not somewhere like Dorton then. Who the fuck has the balls to cart someone into a flat?*

He thought about those in the city—too many of them to count. Shit, he had a hard task ahead trying to narrow the possible locations down.

Oliver continued, "She's slept on and off since. Then she woke needing the toilet. She shit and pissed herself. After that, he told her to have a bath, said if she thought about escaping, it'd be pointless because they were several floors up."

*Damn excellent information.*

"She fell asleep in the bathroom, and when she woke up, she was naked, in the bath, and he was...he was washing her. I can see him doing it— well, just his hand. Freckles on the fingers, hairs on the arms stopping at the wrist—and it doesn't look or feel to me like he gets off on that. She doesn't interest him sexually. She's just someone he needs to wash, make sense?" Oliver rested his cheek on his hand, eyes still closed.

Yeah, that made sense. The previous women hadn't been sexually molested. They hadn't struggled during an attack. No scratches or bruises on their bodies, other than on one woman, and that bruise had been old, yellowed from the passage of time. She hadn't been missing long— what was her name again?—so she'd hurt herself before she'd been abducted. Their fingernails had been pristine. None of the victims had fibres of any kind on them. If they'd had any prior to being dumped, the stream had merrily jostled along and swept them away.

Oliver's breathing grew heavier.

"Don't fall asleep," Langham said. "Try for more. If you can't see more, feel more, try and think if she told you anything else."

46

"She…she said he's soft-spoken, like his voice is a woman's."

*Oh, dear Christ. An out and out nutter.*

"Calls her a good girl. Strokes her cheek. A lot." Oliver sighed, the exhalation rippling as he shuddered. "That's it. That's all I've got." He sat up, bleary-eyed, then stood. "I need a damn Coke."

He looked wretched. Fucking wretched.

Oliver left, and Langham followed, striding past Oliver at the vending machine.

"Come by when you're ready." In the main room, Langham walked through, waving his notes. "Incident room, everyone. We have one hell of a bloody break. Oliver's here."

Heads snapped up. Papers shuffled. Chairs scraped back. The air changed, charged now, everyone knowing that with the mention of Oliver, things had been taken to a new level.

Everyone except Hastings.

"Oliver?" the young officer asked.

"You'll learn, son," Langham said. "You'll learn."

# CHAPTER FIVE

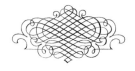

Langham studied Hastings with wry amusement. The officer was so new to this, Langham doubted he'd even seen half the shite the others had seen yet. Hasting stood at the back of the room behind the rows of chairs and watched everyone with an expression of stunned wonderment. The young man's cheeks were ruddy, and his eyes darted about here, there, and every-bloody-where. His jaw was slack, tongue slightly protruding, and if Langham didn't know better, he'd say the man was in a state between panic and shock. Cornered, almost. Like he didn't know what to do for the best, that he had no purpose or wasn't sure what his role was.

*What is he doing on my team again? Who put him in with us?*

There was a buzz in the air, people hyped up, on the verge of getting another bite of information from Oliver. The last snippet he'd given them had been similar to what Langham had just been told. One of the previous women had managed to contact Oliver while she'd been held captive and on drugs, communicating with him between bouts of being out for the count. It had led nowhere, yielded no clues other than her abductor was administering 'medicine' via a syringe and stroking her cheek. She'd gone quiet after contacting Oliver twice, and Oliver had held out hope that she'd get hold of him again. She hadn't. Then her body—or Langham had assumed it was her body—had been found in the stream. He could only hope this latest information didn't fizzle out the same way—that Cheryl's life hadn't fizzled out.

He shifted his gaze from Hastings and found a spot on the far wall, zoning out while everyone settled themselves. The shuffle of notebook pages, the pop of pen lids being pulled off, and the scrape of those infernal metal chair legs on the floor faded into the background.

Those women had been a hard sight to come to terms with. The killer had draped a couple of them over outcropping boulders in the deepest parts of the stream, their feet, hands, and heads in the water, their backs curved. From his vantage point on the bank, Langham had likened them to islands in the stream. The body parts in the water had looked as though the skin would split any second from the pressure of bloating, and the colour...

When the white tents had been erected, the photographers had been and gone, and SOCO had picked over the surrounding area, Langham had returned to watch every one of those women being removed from their final resting places. Some of them had been there a while, faces ballooned, a sick parody of what they'd looked like in life. Eyes missing, some skin sucked on by fishes and whatever the hell else resided in the water. He'd been hard pressed not to puke. He'd thought himself hardened to sights like that, but shit, he'd been wrong.

A sharp bang of the door slamming snapped him out of his reverie. He blinked and stared at Sergeant Villier, who glared back as though he'd purposely called a meeting and hadn't told her. She'd been out and about—bullying people for information, he suspected, what she did best—and he was glad she'd returned in time, if only to save himself the hassle of bringing her up to date with a one-on-one chat later. He hated those. She always interrupted. Then again, she always interrupted in here, too, so what the hell difference did it make whether she attended incident room meetings or not?

"Right," he said, looking at everyone in one sweep then stopping on Hastings, who had remained standing at the back. "Oliver has some information, so as he explains, I'll write it up on the whiteboard."

Oliver stood from his front row seat and ran a hand through his mussed hair. He appeared tired, worn out from being in contact with Cheryl then getting all that data dumped in his head. The dark circles beneath his eyes seemed more pronounced than they'd been ten minutes ago, and two deep gouges bracketed the sides of his mouth where his lips were downturned. Langham turned away to lug the whiteboard across and select a black marker pen.

"Sir?" Hastings said.

Langham swivelled to face him. "Yes?"

"Oliver's that bloke in the newspaper, is he?" Hastings blushed and shifted from foot to foot. "I mean, I've been listening and—"

"That's correct. Any more questions about how Oliver does what he does, ask him later—*if* he's willing to explain. If not, ask someone else who knows. Now, Oliver?"

Oliver repeated the information he'd given Langham. Officers scribbled notes, others narrowed their eyes or frowned. He told them who the victim was and that as far as he was aware, she was still alive.

A question-and-answer session occurred, officers doing what Langham used to do, pressing for more specifics, something Oliver didn't have. Langham allowed it to go on until a muscle spasmed in Oliver's jaw.

"Right, that's enough," Langham said, writing the last note at the end of a long list. Before he forgot, he said, "Someone needs to get a picture of Cheryl for the board." He tapped it with his finger. "And leave Oliver alone. He isn't the bloody oracle. You know how this works. Snippets, and in the past those snippets have held bigger clues than we realised at the time, so now we adopt the pattern we've talked about recently, looking between the lines, writing out all the scenarios that could come up, and seeing if we can find anything, however small, to help us. Thanks, Oliver."

Oliver returned to his seat, slumped down into it, clearly knackered. This one would drain him more, what with him knowing Cheryl. In any other circumstances he wouldn't be allowed on the case—too personal, too raw—but he was the only one who could speak to people with his mind. Apart from Adam, a civilian telepath who'd been a massive help in the Queer Rites case, but since he hadn't called in with any leads, Oliver was on his own. Him taking a back seat unfortunately wasn't an option.

*Poor bastard.*

"Now," Langham said. "Cheryl isn't known for putting herself at risk—although that could be debateable..." He glanced at Oliver, waiting for a look of rebuke. When one wasn't forthcoming, he continued. "Given that she was well aware of women going missing, having helped report it in the local newspaper she works for, we can assume she would have been on her guard. So, with that in mind, we're maybe dealing with a charmer, someone who has the knack of being able to get on your good side without you even noticing he's got evil lurking in his head. Or, and this seems more likely, seeing as Oliver said the man wears a mask, he's a snatch-to-abduct type. Catches these women unaware. I need a background check run on Cheryl, but what I do know—Oliver works with her at said newspaper—she also has a second job. Morning and evening shifts in the café in Morrisons."

Someone groaned. Loud. Long.

"I know, I know." Langham held up a forestalling hand. "We could potentially have thousands of suspects if the killer had his eye on her there, and given that all the victims were taken while walking their dogs on the field opposite... Daunting task, one I wish we didn't have to deal with, but shit happens. You know the drill in situations like this, so I want you all on it. No slacking. We need this bloke caught before Cheryl gets killed. She wasn't at the newspaper this morning. Someone—Hastings—you need to ring Morrisons."

"For...?" Hastings stared.

Langham sighed. *How the fuck do they get through training?* "I just said she also works there.

You need to see how long she's been off work. Were you listening or what?" he snapped.

"Um, sorry, sir."

He gave Hastings a glare that stronger men had withered under. Hastings all but shrivelled up and died. Langham, unable to look at him any longer for fear of seriously hurting him with a caustic barb or two, continued with the briefing.

After answering queries and allotting everyone various tasks, Langham dismissed them. He stood in place while they filed from the room—all except Hastings and Oliver, the latter still in his seat, head bobbing as if he were about ready to drop off.

"Sir?" Hastings said, walking from the back and making a pig's ear of it, tripping on a couple of chairs that jutted from their usual uniformity. He was a bundle of nerves. "Is it all right if I speak to Oliver now?"

Langham glanced at Oliver, torn between letting this copper get his curiosity quieted, and telling him to fuck off if he knew what was good for him. Oliver shook his head, then leant forward to prop his elbows on his knees and cover his face with his hands.

"Oliver's tired," Langham said. "Gets him like that sometimes. Speak to one of the others, preferably not Villier. She's not in Oliver's corner. Doesn't believe in all this 'shit' as she calls it."

"Oh, right, sir." Hastings stood abreast of Langham and stared at Oliver. Hastings' face showed his disappointment. "Only, it's really weird stuff, and I just wanted—" He stopped, nodding to himself. "I'll be off then, sir."

"You do that."

Langham waited until he'd left. For a minute back there he thought he'd have to take Hastings to task, explain with a bit more force that he ought to piss off while the going was good. He hated having to do that, to be seen as the big bad boss, but sometimes, needs must. It seemed Hastings was keen, so that was something, but at times the newbies were *too* keen, more trouble than they were worth.

Langham sat beside Oliver, the chair creaking, wobbling a bit where one of the black rubber feet had come off. "You need to go home."

"I'll be all right in a minute. I just need…some food, maybe a drink." Oliver sat up straighter, blinked several times, then leant forward again to pick up the treats he'd bought from the vending machine. "Sugar. Helps."

Langham stood. "Come on. My office. I need to get some notes down, get my head screwed on straight before I decide what the hell I have to do on this one. Limited officers. It isn't looking good."

Oliver glanced up, his eyes red-rimmed, a little watery. A bag of crisps shook in his hand, the packet rustling. "We've got to find her."

"I know. We'll give it a damn good try. But—"

"I know." Oliver stood. "I fucking know. And even though I don't talk to my mum, my sister, I can't help wondering. What if it was one of them? How would I feel? Just because my mum called me weird all my life, she's still my mum, know what I mean? And I never thought I'd feel like that. Thought I'd cut her out with no trouble. Bloody hell."

Oliver walked away with his head bent, leaving the room with a defeated air about him. The door snapped shut even though he hadn't slammed it, and the white venetian blinds swung across the window insert.

Langham's head spun with his thoughts. Where they hell would they begin? Station undercover officers at the café or send in uniforms to question all customers? No, undercover would be better. Less chance of the bastard—if he even used the supermarket—becoming aware they were on to him, drawing closer. If he saw a police presence, he might change venue, and that was all they bloody needed. Now they had such a solid lead, they'd have to run with it as best they could, hoping the killer stuck to old ground as he had in the past.

Who would go and interview the newspaper staff? He would, but Oliver would probably insist on going with him, saying he had a better chance to get them to talk, to know if they were lying by looking at their faces. But some people could control their features, rarely a telling tic or micro-expression to be seen.

And now there was Oliver and his admission about his mother and sister. Langham never thought Oliver would have worried about them, not after how they'd acted towards him when he was growing up.

"Jesus wept," he said quietly. "This is one hell of a nightmare."

He strode through the main office, waylaid by various officers, responding to questions he was thankfully able to answer. Yes, you need to check into Cheryl's background, see if she is actually missing. No, I don't doubt Oliver for a second. Yes, you need to send plain-clothed officers out to Morrisons, see if the staff noticed anyone lurking about the past few nights by the field. No, I haven't got a bloody clue where Wilkes is.

Back in his office, Oliver chomping on crisps, Langham shut the door and leant against it.

*God help anyone who knocks now…*

His phone rang.

"I don't need this at the moment." Langham gritted his teeth.

"Better answer that," Oliver said.

Langham sighed. "Fuck it." He walked to the desk then snatched up the phone. "Langham."

"It's Hastings, sir."

"Go on." *Please don't let him ask an imbecilic question…*

"There's no missing person's report on Miss Witherspoon, so I telephoned the newspaper and Morrisons. She didn't show up at either place. Unusual for her, Morrisons said, because she always calls in if she's ill. So I ran a check and found her parents. They live in Scotland—doubt they'd even know she was missing unless Miss

Witherspoon got in contact every day, and seeing as she hasn't been reported as being gone..."

"Yep, yep. Good work. Let Villier know what you've found. She'll give you further direction." Langham dropped the phone onto the cradle without saying goodbye. He couldn't be arsed and wasn't in the mood for niceties. He'd felt sorry for Hastings at the first meeting, but he'd got on his nerves in the last. The man was out of his depth—stupid of him to be on loan in their office at the moment, supposedly learning how things worked in this department. What—did he have a view to working on Langham's squad? Did the powers that be see something in Hastings worth nurturing? Not fucking likely, unless he pulled his finger out and stopped acting so damn wet.

The phone rang again. He picked up. "*What?*"

"Hastings, sir."

*Holy Jesus fuck...* "Yes?"

"You didn't let me finish my last call, sir."

Langham closed his eyes and bared his teeth. He was seriously on edge now, wanting to sort through the information and see what they needed to do next. The thought of Cheryl being bathed in bleach, that her time might be running out, chilled him to the bone. Talking to Hastings, hand-holding him, wasn't a job he had the inclination to throw himself into.

"Right. Get on with it then, Hastings." *This had better be good...*

"Someone else visited the newspaper asking after her."

"And?"

"And it wasn't one of us, sir."

"What?"

"Male civilian asking questions. How long she'd been off work, stuff like that. Newspaper editor said he'd acted a bit furtive."

"When was this?" Langham grabbed a pen and tapped it on the table.

"About half an hour ago."

Langham's breath came out in an almighty whoosh. He put the phone down and lifted his jacket off the back of his chair.

"Going somewhere?" Oliver stood, more alert now.

"Yep. Someone's been at the newspaper asking questions."

"Oh? Must have been after I left. It's been quiet there all morning until...until Cheryl got hold of me."

"Half an hour ago." Langham shrugged into his jacket. "You coming?"

"Yep." Oliver rubbed one eye with a knuckle.

"They got CCTV there?" Langham walked to his door then pulled it open.

"Yeah. Had to. We get all kinds of nutters showing up, angry about the stories."

"Good. Because I'm going to need to see it." *And please let the bastard who was nosing around earlier be young, blond, and with green eyes.*

# CHAPTER SIX

David stared at her from the bedroom doorway, taking a moment to think. He'd go for a walk at some point, clear the cobwebs, get back to being totally focused. Perhaps come back and write in his diary. That little book was a Godsend. Like, as soon as he started writing, all the angst went away, spilling onto the page.

Cheryl was asleep now. She'd need some more drugs soon. He'd given her a small dose, just enough so she would get a solid hour or two of sleep while he sat on the sofa and meditated, waiting for Mr Clever to tell him it was The Time. He always liked that bit. He got to be someone totally different, didn't he, or perhaps who he was supposed to be. Yeah, that was it. That was what his personal journey was all about. Becoming himself. How many women would he have to kill in order to be his true self all the time? Or was the killing ritual the only thing that enabled him to *be* himself?

He was discovering more every day, and the answers to his questions would come. *Rome wasn't built in a day*—Mr Clever had told him that, and seeing as Mr Clever *was* such a clever man, David just had to trust in his voice and do as he was being told. It would all come out in the wash, like people were fond of saying. But things didn't always come out in the wash, did they?

He shoved that thought aside, knowing if he chased it, he'd end up in a mess, worrying about things he shouldn't concern himself with. And being a mess might fuck with what he was doing, and he couldn't have that.

He took the mask off, regretting its loss—it had become a part of him, the condensation inside disguising any tears that might want to fall—yet at the same time he was relieved to have some clean air on his skin. Well, cleaner now that Cheryl had been bleached and the air freshener had done exactly what it claimed it would: *Floral Breeze doesn't just mask odours, it takes them away!*

He went into his bedroom next to hers to place the mask back in his bedside drawer. He stroked it. The cheeks were as soft as the women's—he closed his eyes and imagined the ritual had started already, that he was doing what he always did before they were snuffed out for good. The familiar feeling of The Time came then, and he snapped his eyes open. He went to the bathroom to check on the knickers, the only thing of Cheryl's he hadn't put in the washing machine. He stared into the sink, pleased to see all traces of the mess had gone—bleach, he loved it, so good at getting rid of stains and stenches—so unplugged the stopper then rinsed them through. After squeezing them out, he draped them over the radiator then walked out into the hallway to turn up the heating so they'd dry quicker.

He stood with eyes closed, his back against the wall. Waited. Held his breath, his lungs screaming for him to release it. What he'd anticipated came then. The grind and squeak of the pipes getting hot. It gave him a settled feeling. He'd always liked that noise. It reminded him of his childhood when he'd huddled in the corner with Sally, while his parents had argued. The pipes in their old house had been dreadful, loud, but they'd helped drown out the voices—except the one in his head. How had he gone so many years without knowing Mr Clever's name? Why had he never thought to ask what it was before now?

*"Because you thought I was you, didn't you, David?"*

"Yes, I did."

*"While the knickers dry, go and get Sally."*

David returned to his bedroom. The tumble dryer in the kitchen worked its warming magic on Cheryl's clothes, the hum of it filtering through. Sally sat on his bed where she always was until The Time. Two fluffy brown scatter cushions propped her up, the polyester fibres stroking her arms with the help of a breeze coming through the window. He shouldn't have left that open and strutted over to it. Closed it tight and locked it. None of the women had ever tried to jump out— but then he hadn't given them the chance to.

He moved back onto the bed, picked Sally up. She sat in his lap quite nicely, her chubby legs sticking out and resting directly on his thighs. She'd been with him through so many things, and if he ever lost her, he'd be heartbroken. It wasn't often people found themselves still in possession of their childhood friend two decades later, was it.

He ran his hand down Sally's springy blonde hair, the nylon feel and smell still the same as ever. She stared ahead, plastic arms by her sides, fingertips touching the red-flowered material of her sleeveless summer dress. The cord handle in her back, once a crisp white ring but now an aged cream, dug into the top of his belly, and he shifted her forward so he could pull it and listen.

A melody tinkled out of her, full of sweet, high-pitched notes, the tones soothing him. He closed his eyes and let the music wash over him, bringing with it memories of the past when Sally had been there for him with the women. She'd watched from her position against the wall as he'd done his thing and she'd played her tune, never letting him down, always saying, "Goodnight!" in her chirpy little voice at the right moment.

"I love you, Sally."

"Goodnight!"

"Yes, it's goodnight for now, but I think I'll be coming back to get you soon."

It was The Time. David was surprised at that, but he shouldn't have been, not with what he knew. It was Friday, and he needed to make Cheryl go *home-home* today. He couldn't risk leaving her over the weekend when he went to work. And Monday might be too late. If that Oliver fella managed to speak to her or she to him…

No, she had to go now. Sad, because he'd enjoyed bathing her, making her so clean her hair had squeaked as he'd washed it. The bleach had turned it a nasty colour, though—nasty because it was an orangey-yellow blonde. He didn't like blondes.

Another reason why Cheryl had to go.

Sally was in place beside Cheryl's bedroom door, a prime position so she could see it all and not miss a thing. Awake and naked, Cheryl crouched at one end of the mattress, squished into the corner. She'd bent her legs and hugged them,

65

resting her chin on top of her knees as David had walked in. Her heels covered her private garden. He was glad about that. He didn't want to see the horrible redness of it. The hairy, horrible redness.

She stared at Sally as though she was a piece of shit.

That wasn't pleasant to see.

"Sally is here to let you listen to her wonderful music," David said in a voice he'd begun using with woman number two, a soft, melodious one much like Sally's tune. "Smile at Sally, Cheryl."

Cheryl smiled, albeit a tentative one, but it was enough. At least she hadn't disobeyed him. And maybe she liked Sally and just didn't know how to express it.

He glanced at his dolly, trying to see her through Cheryl's eyes. All right, she wasn't the prettiest, what with her face being a swirl of melted plastic where she'd found herself in the fireplace after his father had thrown her there. Her eyes sagged downwards, just like his mask, and her mouth was a ragged stretch of its former self. David had rescued her, though, pulling her out of the flames and rolling her in the rug like he'd been taught when the firemen had visited the school for a chat about safety. The back of her hair hadn't caught—her blonde hair—and he realised then, with sudden clarity, that was why he didn't bring blondes home.

There was room for only one in his life, and that was Sally.

"I want you to take some more medicine so you'll be in that place you need to be." He approached Cheryl with a loaded syringe. "Everything will be okay soon."

She tried to lose herself in the wall, pushing back with her palms splayed on it, fingers bent at the knuckles, spiders' leg joints. He waited while she came to the realisation she wasn't getting anywhere, him patient, yet longing, to go into the bathroom and start dressing for the occasion. A few seconds passed with Cheryl whimpering, then she flopped out one arm, offering her vein to him.

"There we are," he said quietly. "So good. Aren't you so good?" He waited for her nod, then, "Yes, you are."

He did the necessary and eased the needle in, squeezing the magic potion into her body. This draft would keep her lucid yet pliable enough for him to manage her, to not have to worry that she'd lash out or run amok in his flat. She dropped her head back and stared at him, but not seeing him clearly, he reckoned. He'd be a blurred shape, his mask possibly more frightening than it usually was, all skewed mouth and hanging eyes. Smooth cheeks.

He threw the syringe in the waste basket on his way out, heading for the bathroom. Pausing at the radiator, he picked up the knickers and, satisfied they were dry, lifted them to his face. Because she'd been a dirty girl and messed them, they didn't smell like the other women's. That annoyed him, but he controlled himself and remained calm as he stepped into them, pulling them up over his jeans.

Back in the bedroom, he stood in front of Cheryl and curtseyed, then did a pirouette so she could see how he looked in her underwear. She widened her eyes, her facial expression showing her disgust, her terror.

"You don't like them on me?" He stepped closer so she could get a better view. She hadn't been able to see them properly, that was it.

She moved her head, but he wasn't sure whether that indicated a yes or a no.

"Answer me, there's a good girl. Aren't they lovely?"

She slurred out a yes and gave a definite nod.

"I think so, too." He reached out and swiped her white bra from the top of her clean clothes pile on the floor. With the practise he'd had, he was able to put it on over his polo shirt quickly, enjoying the way the cups stood out. "And this? How do I look in this?"

She nodded again, faster this time, and her lips twitched.

He took that for a smile.

"I like wearing girly clothes," he said, impressed with how his voice had sounded.

Lilting.

He sat on the mattress, glancing at Sally to make sure she was still watching. She was, so he turned his attention to Cheryl. He stroked her cheek with the backs of his fingers. Her skin was divine, like nectarines, or maybe even the velvet of the sofa they'd had when he was a child. Sally had always liked that sofa, although they hadn't sat on it often. Sitting on it was a treat, something to be relished, because it meant his parents were getting along and he didn't have to stay in his room to avoid their spats.

Cheryl blinked, and a faint tic pulsed beneath one eye.

She didn't like him touching her.

They never did. All they had to do was like it, and he wouldn't have to send them *home-home*. All they had to do was enjoy him stroking their cheeks, tell him they hadn't had enough of him, and he would be happy. Instead, they'd all cringed, all hated him, and it made him do what he did.

"Mmmm, this is nice," he said. "Say it's nice, Cheryl."

She opened her mouth, flapped her lips, but no words came out. He hadn't given her *that* much medicine—she ought to be able to answer.

"Tell me it's nice, Cheryl." He didn't sound so melodious this time, more like his other self. He licked the sweat from above his top lip to remind himself of just who he was now. Applied more pressure to his cheek strokes.

She did an outright wince this time, and a knot of anger bunched in his belly. He'd try one more time to get her to speak, and if she didn't…

"Tell me it's nice, Cheryl."

"S'nice."

"Tell me you want me to keep doing it."

"Keep doin' it."

"No."

He stood abruptly and stared down at her. She appeared confused, deep frown lines fucking up her brow, and that got him happy. He pranced about the small space on tiptoes, arms out by his sides, and listened to Sally's tune playing in his head. Soon he'd pull the cord in her back and let her music fill the room for real, but for now she'd be content to just sit and take it all in. Sally was a good girl, the only one who liked him stroking her cheek, what was left of her hair.

Euphoria spread through him, his steps lighter. He closed his eyes and let the music take him away, to that place where everything was fine and nothing mattered except what he was feeling. He was aware, deep in the back of his mind, that Cheryl would be watching him, wondering what the hell he was doing and why, but her opinion wasn't something he cared for. He didn't think he cared anyway.

The imaginary music came to an end, Sally's perky "Goodnight!" filling his head, and he smiled, slowed his steps, then stopped. He remained where he was, eyes still closed, and lowered his arms to his sides. Took a moment or two for himself, to soak in the warm feeling of being exactly where he needed to be.

He snapped his eyes open and found himself facing the door, Cheryl's gaze hot on his back. She could stare all she liked. Maybe she was secretly admiring her bra and knickers, how they fitted him so well. Wondering why they'd never looked as good on her. That would be nice.

Mr Clever had questioned him once as to why he put them over his own clothes, why he didn't strip and wear them against his skin. He hadn't been able to answer because he didn't *know* why. He'd thought about it, though, but nothing had been forthcoming. Mr Clever then suggested he was entertaining his feminine side while at the same time retaining his persona as a man, but David didn't know if that was right either. He *did* know that he liked wearing them, and that explanation ought to be enough. He shouldn't have to explain.

"Why do you think I like wearing your things, Cheryl?" He gave Sally a knowing look because they all answered the same way.

"Dunnow," Cheryl said.

Ah, she hadn't called him a freak, a weirdo, a nutcase.

Interesting.

"Aren't you curious?" *I am. I wouldn't wear them as my other self. I'd call any man wearing them a nasty name.*

"Your biznizz," she said, voice slurred.

Her response threw him. His business? He quickly turned to face her, to catch any facial expression that belied her words, but her vacant stare was glued to Sally, and she exhibited blankness, as though nothing mattered anymore.

The next phase could begin then.

71

He sat on the mattress again, leaning down, and pushed his lips out through the mask hole so they were millimetres from her cheek. "Have you had enough yet, Cheryl?"

"Enough o' wot?" she mumbled, eyes drifting closed.

"Of me."

"Had nuff o' this," she said.

Oh. Right. She hadn't had enough of *him?*

"What about me, Cheryl?" he singsonged. "Have you had enough of *me* yet?"

*"Remember your mother, David?"* Mr Clever asked. *"I've had enough of you, you little bastard. Get the fuck out of my sight!"*

Cheryl shook her head.

David held his breath. Frowned, unsure what to do or say. He tried a different angle. "Do you want to leave here, Cheryl?"

She sniffed. "Want to go home."

"I see." His hot breath bounced off her cheek. "Home to where you live, or *home-home*, the place where we all go in the end?"

"Where I live." She'd sounded like a slowing gramophone record.

"Oh. That's a shame. It isn't possible, good girl. Mr Clever wants you to go *home-home*."

Her eyelashes fluttered. A tear spilled.

He withdrew sharply and stood. Went to the chest of drawers and picked up a new syringe full of medicine. He'd have to visit The Stick again soon. His supply was almost gone. He gazed at Sally and smiled, letting her know she must play

72

her part now. He'd swear she wiggled her toes in excitement. He scooped her up and stood beside the mattress.

"Now, Cheryl," he breathed. "You can go home."

He handed her the syringe. She held it in a loose-fingered grip, staring at it as more tears fell. She appeared uncomprehending, as though not knowing what the syringe was doing there, *how* it had got there. Perhaps she was going through a strange spell, the drug doing weird things to her. Maybe she'd be back to normal in a minute—well, as normal as she could be in the circumstances— and she'd understand exactly what she had to do next.

"If you don't take your medicine, it will get worse," he said. "Mr Clever might tell me to do other things to you, and then you'll use the syringe gladly."

She lifted it. Sat upright and leant forward, her head seemingly too heavy for her neck. He stared at the cords standing out in her throat and wondered how much effort she had to put in to keep her chin from dropping to her chest. She jabbed the needle between her toes like a true heroin addict who knew where to hide those telling holes from the suspecting eyes of family members and friends. Squeezed the syringe until all the medicine disappeared.

"There," he said, voice quiet and even. "That wasn't so difficult, was it?"

He pulled Sally's cord and smiled as the music played. Cheryl took the needle out, rested back, and closed her eyes, the syringe falling from her grasp. He stared until the song was almost complete then ran with Sally to the door, going out into the hallway and closing it a little, positioning Sally halfway up the jamb so she peeked into the bedroom.

"Goodnight!" Sally said.

# CHAPTER SEVEN

L angham and Oliver walked into the newspaper office. The bolshy editor ordered Oliver to let him in on the gossip, give him something for tomorrow's edition.

"No gossip at this time," Langham said, holding a palm up.

The editor opened his mouth to protest, and Langham levelled one of his stares at him that said: *No further orders. No further prods for a scoop.*

"Tell me what you know about Cheryl's absence," Langham said.

"She wasn't due in to work the past couple of days, so her not being here wasn't a concern." The ed shrugged. "This morning, I was pissed off she hadn't shown because we had a shitload of makeup and feminine hygiene articles that had needed going over, and Cheryl had been chosen to do it. Her not coming in meant Colin, the dopey little shyster, had had to take over, and what the hell does Colin know about makeup?"

Langham suspected quite a bit, going by Colin's blush, the remnants of eyeliner, and the quick glance from where he sat in the corner at his desk.

"I need to see the CCTV," Langham said.

In the editor's office, it was brought up on screen. The footage showed a man—late twenties, black suit, white shirt, grey tie, floppy dark hair, nothing like the bloke they were after—come bursting into reception like he'd been chased up the stairs. The woman behind the desk tried to stop him from going through to the offices, but he pushed past her, raising his voice and saying he had to see Cheryl and make sure she was all right.

"Bloody lunatic," the editor said. "Almost made me shit myself, the way he stormed in here. Thought he was some nutter at first—we get a lot of those—but once he calmed down a bit and explained... He reckoned she was supposed to have met him for a date and hadn't turned up. Couldn't see it myself. Cheryl usually goes for the more laid-back type. Casual, modern clothes and all that. You know, T-shirts and jeans. This bloke? Suit and tie? Nah."

Langham and Oliver left after that.

Now, Langham sat at his desk. Evening had arrived at one hell of a pace, darkness falling without notice—one minute the late afternoon sun had been thinking about going to bed, the next it had disappeared and the moon was wide awake.

Oliver dozed in the chair opposite, hands clasped over his stomach.

Langham mulled things over. What if the *killer* was Cheryl's usual type? What if he'd appealed to her in his sweatshirt and jeans while she'd been out walking her dog? She could have taken a fancy to him and let him get close. Totally forgotten about a murderer on the loose, taking women and offing them. He'd got hold of her dog, then her...

There was a lot to think about. Officers, the new shift, would shortly be sent out to walk the banks of the stream to check for her. The previous victims had been dumped in close locations—well, close on a map but quite far apart on foot. Still, the killer had chosen to keep them all together, so to speak. Langham brought up a map of the area on his computer. He studied it and the surrounding area. Around the section of stream the killer favoured was a forest. He had to be using that as cover when carrying his victims to the water.

Beyond the forest and on one side of the stream stood a housing estate, but farther up, where the stream broadened and headed out of the city, were farmers' fields.

*So he may well live on that housing estate. Parks up on that road there then carries them through the woods. Might be worth putting a few undercovers out there tonight.*

He scribbled that down to remind him to do that in a bit, then changed his mind and went into the main office, instructing Villier, who hadn't gone home yet, damn her, to get that sorted. She huffed, her cheeks ballooning with her expelled breath, but she must have been too tired to employ her usual waspishness because she offered no further protest.

Back in his office, Langham thought of all the high-rises, whether there were even any on that estate. As he recalled, there weren't, unless he included the two-storey flats.

"No, Cheryl had said she was several floors up," he muttered.

He studied the map some more, casting his gaze to the left—to an estate that housed mainly council tenants. Plenty of high-rises there, cheap accommodation taking up less space, piss-stinking rat-holes. And many of them were. Drugs and prostitution were rife there, the main street through the estate riddled with women strolling up and down the pavement after dark. No nice kids out playing there—fuck no—and if kids *were* out, they wouldn't be playing and they weren't nice. Selling small folds of crack on the corners, more like, their main customers the sex workers themselves. Anything to get the women through the night, through the customers. Then there was The Stick, a patch of ground tucked away behind the railway bridge, where drugs were sold and taken and the homeless huddled around the proverbial empty oil drums filled with pitiful excuses for fires.

*She'd mentioned medicine. A syringe.*

Langham got up and went back to the main room. Stood leaning against the wall, watching everyone working. His mind spun with information, him wanting to grab at snippets that were too fast for him to catch—snippets he knew were significant but, because he didn't know what the hell they were, he couldn't figure out what he needed to latch on to. Then one of those snippets drifted out of the crowd, zooming around, screeching that it needed someone, anyone, to take note and listen.

*Jesus. Fucking hell, why didn't I see that before?*

"Anyone been to The Stick yet?" he called out.

Mumbles of: *No time... Thought someone else was doing it... Sorry, sir...*

"Well, someone needs to. She's being drugged. Best to strike The Stick off our list so we can think on where else this fucker's getting his stuff from."

The doctors' surgeries and hospitals hadn't thrown up any leads. Amazingly, no young man had the combination of blond hair, green eyes, and the tendency to only work on weekends. He hadn't ruled those places out, though. This man might well work during the week, and until Langham had proof that he didn't, he'd have to go on the assumption that the killer held down a full-time job—or wasn't even employed at all.

He moved to turn back to his office, but another thought had him pausing. "Anyone out at the field opposite Morrisons?"

More varied answers: *Not sure, sir... Didn't see the point when he has someone abducted already, sir... Didn't think he'd bother going for another one while he has Witherspoon, sir...*

He sighed.

*If one more person calls me sir tonight...*

"Well, send a couple out anyway!" he shouted, frustrated and ready to punch the first unfortunate sod to get in his face. "Specifically have a pair of you on the estate behind the forest. Go out in casual clothes, walk around like you live there. Get a feel for the fucking place. Stand around at the point where the estate meets the forest, chat like you're just taking a breather, and have a good gander at the route he might be taking once he enters the forest. While he has Witherspoon, now's the chance to go there without him copping on to us."

"Who should go?" someone asked.

"Fuck me sideways. Think about it. Shitty estate, filled with the younger generation. So, two of you who could pass for twenty-somethings, all right? Get clothes from the undercover store. Just get on with it."

He stormed back to his office. Oliver was awake, staring at the wall behind Langham's desk, his face pale, his hands shaking.

*Jesus fucking Christ, she's made contact...*

Langham went to his chair and sat, though God knew how he'd manage to stay put. Oliver continued to study the wall, his eyes glazed. He fiddled with the zip of his lightweight jacket.

Langham swallowed. Waited. Swallowed again.

As Oliver twitched, Langham bit his tongue. Oliver narrowed his eyes then sighed, as if he tried to understand, to make sense of the data.

"He's got a doll," Oliver said. "A fucking creepy-arsed doll."

Langham leant forward, clasped his hands. Stared at the gouge in the desk, at the biscuit crumb and dust he'd failed to get rid of.

A doll. What the hell? *Were* they dealing with a woman? No, no, they couldn't be—unless that woman had the ability to grow stubble. So what man had the need for a doll? *Why* did he have a doll?

"It's staring at her," Oliver said. "Watching while he...he dances to this...this horrible music. It tinkles. Like a music box, except it isn't right. It's just not right. Creepy. Makes me think of horror movies, the bit where the music starts just before something nasty happens. He's got Cheryl's bra and knickers on over his clothes."

*What?*

So they had a man who liked wearing women's clothing, spoke like a lady, and had a doll. What,

81

did he think he *was* a woman, was that it? Was he transitioning?

"He kept stroking her cheek," Oliver said, "calling her a good girl and telling her she had to go home."

Langham wanted to ask when, and why Cheryl was allowed home and the other women weren't. He kept his mouth shut, though, shifting his gaze to the open packet of biscuits he hadn't put back in the drawer. He took one out. Nibbled on it. Stale.

Oliver sighed. "Except it isn't home. He means death."

*Oh God...*

"He gave her some medicine, but she didn't take it. Didn't inject herself. She put the needle between her toes and squeezed the drug into the mattress." Oliver paused, waiting as though he was being spoken to or he was deciphering images. "Cheryl? Is that you?"

*She's talking. She's got through!* Langham resisted punching the air. His heart rate sped up, adrenaline streaking out of the starting gate and romping down the stretch. It sent him momentarily giddy, and he inhaled and exhaled a few deep breaths to calm himself.

"You what?" Oliver said. "Say that again. Right...yes, try and keep talking to me. I'll help you through this, tell you what to do. Yes, you did the right thing with the needle. Pretend you're asleep, okay? Whatever happens, just do that—unless you can get away safely. Don't try anything stupid, though, all right? Let him do his thing."

Langham tossed his biscuit on the desk then drew a notepad across and wrote everything down.

"No, he won't hurt you," Oliver said. "Remember the others? None of them had been hurt. None...touched like *that*. He's not interested in getting thrills via sex, so stop panicking about it. What? Repeat that for me... No, I don't know why he'd want to wear your things..." He sighed. "Right, so he hasn't worn them before now? Okay, fine. Just... No, don't panic. Stay where you are, do what you're doing. We're all working on this. We'll get to you before it goes much further. We'll find you. So long as you can stay in contact with me, we'll find you."

*That's a promise you shouldn't be making. We might find her all right, but it could be too late. We know her destination, know where she'll bloody end up, but we need to find her before the water finishes her off.*

"Fuck!" Oliver said. "Cheryl? Are you there?"

Langham looked up at Oliver, who snapped out of his trance and smacked the side of his fist onto the desk.

"She's gone. Fucking hell, she's gone." Oliver stared at him, clearly trying hard to keep his emotions in check. "We have to..." He jumped up. Paced. Head bent, hand up to his mouth. "We have to get out there. Do something. *Find* her."

They'd been through this before. And, as before, Langham told him they were doing all they could, and haring out into the night with no idea where they needed to be wasn't going to help. And shit, earlier today, he'd ordered a couple of young officers to hang about on that estate. He quickly put a call through to the main office, getting someone to get them back for now. The last thing they needed was uniforms prowling around down there and scaring the man off. If he spotted them, he might change his dump site, then they'd be well and truly fucked in finding Cheryl. The two he'd told to wear civilian clothing could stay.

"I *hate* this part!" Oliver flung himself into his chair so it scooted backwards and barged into a filing cabinet. "I feel so *helpless!*"

"I know you do," Langham said. "So do I, but we have no bloody idea where she is." He brought Oliver up to speed on what had been happening while he'd dozed. "So we've got things covered. Nothing else we can do."

The phone rang. Langham leant over the desk to answer it.

"The staff at Morrisons café have been interviewed, sir."

"What the hell are you still doing here, Hastings? Didn't you hand everything over on shift change?" Langham asked.

"I did, but I've got caught up in this and I...I'm not tired. Thought I may as well stay until I am."

"Right." *Good lad.* "Got anything for me?"

"Seems that man who was asking questions at the newspaper also went to Morrisons. He eats there most mornings, apparently, with some other bloke."

"Okay." *Who is that fucker?* "Anything else?"

"Yes, sir. We think we have him."

"What, you think you know who he is?"

"No. As in, we have him downstairs. He'd been to the field this evening, asking people questions, whether they'd seen Cheryl and whatnot. And he found her dog."

"What!" Jesus! Why hadn't the uniforms found the fucking dog? Had they even gone out there yet? "Where is he?"

"Interview room two, sir, waiting for you."

Langham sat across the table from the same man who had been the star of the newspaper CCTV footage. He looked shaken up—that or he was coming down from an adrenaline rush. He'd certainly been busy today, gallivanting about, poking his nose into things he shouldn't. Langham briefly entertained the idea he might be the one they were looking for but dismissed the thought. Although he could wear a wig and contact lenses to make people think he was blond and green-eyed, it didn't sit right. Didn't *feel* right. This man didn't appear to have it in him to abduct women. Bit of a wet blanket. Still, he'd been wrong before and decided to wait and see what the interview brought up.

"So, explain to me again, Conrad, why you've been asking questions," Langham said.

Oliver watched through the two-way glass behind him, ready to pick up on anything that might present its ugly self.

Conrad Leddings sighed. "I was supposed to meet Cheryl for a date. I've liked her for ages. We exchanged numbers, and I thought...I thought she liked me."

"Where did you meet?"

"She works in the café in Morrisons. I see her on the early morning shift. You know, breakfast and whatnot. Does evenings an' all."

"Go on."

"But she didn't turn up for the date. I went home, thought nothing much about it except maybe she didn't like me after all. Okay, being honest, I was well gutted, but I can't force her to like me. Then the next day I went to Morrisons, and she wasn't there. I knew something was wrong. She's always there, and what with that weirdo going around taking women... Please, there's something going on."

*It isn't him.*

"Yes, something's most definitely going on." Langham waited for the shocked, panicked look to clear from Conrad's face, then he went on. "Tell me what you've done today."

"It isn't me, I swear to God it isn't me!" He clenched then unclenched his fists on the table, as though fighting to remain calm. He definitely had the air of panic about him, the air of a concerned person, not that of a killer wanting to involve himself in the investigation on the police side.

86

"All right." Langham cleared his throat. "So, tell me what you've done today."

Conrad bounced one leg, and his body shook. His mouth downturned as though he held back tears. "I said to my friend something was up, and he said she was probably ill, and I thought he might be right, because people do get ill, don't they, but something inside told me different."

Langham tilted his head, raising his eyebrows so the man stopped waffling and told him what he damn well wanted to hear.

"Anyway," Conrad said, "I went to her house— she'd told me where she lived after we'd arranged our date. No one in. I knocked on the doors either side of her place and asked the neighbours if they'd seen her."

"And had they?" *Yes, taking her dog out for a walk, as usual.* Uniforms had already been there and found this out.

"Yes. When she went out to take her dog for a walk."

"And then what did you do?" *You went to the newspaper.*

"I went to the newspaper. She hadn't called in sick. So then I went to Morrisons, asked if *they'd* seen her, and no one had. She hadn't been there this morning—she always waits on us, *always* serves us breakfast and a pot of tea and..." Conrad swallowed. Blinked a few times.

"Carry on."

"I got to thinking. And I waited until this evening to go the field and ask people there if they'd seen her. One man had—the night her neighbours had last seen her taking the dog out. Said he'd seen her about eight. He didn't seem weird, not the kind who'd take a woman, and anyway, he had his kid with him. Little girl of about seven."

*People with kids and family lives still take women and kill them, Conrad.* "Then what did you do?"

"I went over to where the forest starts. I don't know why, just felt the need to do it. I walked through for a bit, not far, and saw this lump. Made my guts roll over, I can tell you, like I just knew something was up with that. I went closer and…oh God, it was a dog. Big thing, long-haired. And I knew it was hers, you know?"

*Yes, I know.* "Then you called the police."

Conrad nodded. Leg still bouncing. Body still shaking. "They'll be looking for her now, won't they? Please tell me they'll be looking."

"Oh, yes. They'll be out there all night."

"Oh, thank God. No one seemed to want to listen to me. No one seemed to *care*, not even David."

"Who's David?"

"My friend. I meet him for breakfast most mornings."

"Good sort, is he, this David?"

"Yes, yes, he is. Nice man." Conrad absently stared at the tabletop. "So will you let me know? I mean, if things…if she's…" His lip wobbled.

"We will."

"And that psychic bloke? The one who's always in the paper. Is he on the case?"

"He is."

"Thank you, God," Conrad said, gazing at the ceiling.

"And believe me," Langham said, "if the 'psychic bloke' gets anything, we'll be on it immediately. We'll find the man responsible, no doubt about it." *We just don't know when.*

"But what about Cheryl? Will you find her before he...before...?"

*I fucking hope so.*

Langham gave a tight smile, deciding not to answer that particular question. He stood. "We'll be in touch at some point, Mr Leddings. I have to go now, sort through some things, but I'll send another detective on my team down to go through this with you again. You know, a full description of the man with his daughter, things like that. Maybe get an identikit done of him. That'll be a help in eliminating him from our enquiries should we come across him ourselves at some point. I appreciate your help, but it would be better if you didn't go around doing any detective work yourself now. Stay out of it—you wouldn't want us thinking it was you, would you?"

Conrad shook his head. "No, no. It isn't me. No, I wouldn't want that."

*Good job I don't think you're our man then, isn't it.*

Langham gave a curt nod and left the room.

# CHAPTER EIGHT

Leaning on the bedroom doorjamb, David waited twenty minutes for the medicine to kick in. By the deepness of Cheryl's breathing, she was ready for transportation. It was earlier than he usually went out, but that was okay, he had yet to wash her so that would take up some minutes.

He tweaked the bra strap and smiled as it snapped back onto his shoulder. Did the same with the side of the knickers. That snap wasn't as satisfactory, but no matter.

It was time to bathe her in bleach again, get as much of this place off her as he could. If anything remained after that, the stream would hopefully take care of it. And it had with the other women, so he shouldn't have thought 'hopefully'. The stream *would* sort things. It was his accomplice, the element that put the cherries firmly on top of the cakes he made. He smiled at thinking of himself as a baker. Maybe when he got home later he'd make a batch of biscuits and sit and eat them on his bed with Sally.

He bent down to pick her up. Took her into the bathroom. Lowered the toilet lid then sat her on top so she faced the bath and could watch everything he did. Then he returned to collect Cheryl. She was easy to carry, so light. She still smelt of bleach from her last bath, although the scent had faded a bit, the aroma of sleep and inactivity masking it.

He put her in the bath, the beautiful smell of new bleach in the hot water filling his nose. It reminded him of swimming pools, of the strong stench of chlorine he'd loved so much as a kid when they'd had lessons in the school pool. He let her go, the level low enough that her face didn't go under but high enough that it reached her collarbones. Satisfied she was submerged adequately, he bent her legs then placed his hand on her head. Took a second to fully feel the tickle of her hair on his skin. Her brittle, bleach-ruined blonde hair. He pushed her beneath the water so her head was completely under. Every bit of her needed a bleaching, so he kept his hand on her head and stared at his watch until fifteen seconds had passed.

The medicine had rendered her so out of it she didn't struggle, didn't even know she was in the bloody bath. Didn't appear to be breathing. He eased her up again and straightened her legs, putting her feet flat against the end so she didn't slip. At this point he usually let them remain under the water until they went *home-home*, then pulled them back out so he could hold one of their eyes open with finger and thumb to check for the grey clouds over the blue iris moon. This time he wanted to do it differently. Mr Clever hadn't said he couldn't, and that was always a good sign.

"It's healthy to have a bit of a change, isn't it, Sally?" He glanced over his shoulder while he knelt.

Sally gave him her vacant, skew-eyed stare. He turned back to face the bath and took the soap from the ceramic pig holder on the corner and created froth in his hands. He washed her face, paying particular attention to her cheek where he'd stroked it. Some bubbles went up her nose as she inhaled, and he was glad. It saved him the trouble of scrubbing up there with a cotton bud. He rinsed her, replaced the soap, then selected a metal nail file. David chose the pointed end to scrape beneath her fingernails, doing the same with those on her toes. He used the green scouring pad of a kitchen sponge to scrub behind her ears and in the creases of her neck. It took half an hour to clean her thoroughly, inside and out.

Next, he tugged out the plug and watched the water drain away. Once it had all gone and she lay with her head at an awkward angle now she wasn't buoyant, he reached for the shower head. He switched the water on, sluicing her down so no scum from her nails or fibres from his flat clung to her. Happy she was sanitised, he shut off the water and left her to dry naturally.

In his bedroom, he donned his black boiler suit and tucked his hair into a navy-blue beanie.

*"I don't think she'll wake, David, but you might want to take precautions."*

David didn't think she would wake up either but folded his mask into four and slipped it into his pocket along with a capped syringe of medicine. Mr Clever had been right with his advice. You could never be too cocky, too sure of yourself, and sometimes people did the strangest things. Cheryl might not be like the others. She might wake up on the way to his car or at least stir as she hung over his shoulder, and if he could jab her with the needle before she woke fully and possibly created a fuss, that would be grand.

He looked at himself in the mirror beside his bedroom door, pleased at his calm expression, his blank eyes. Even if someone stopped him when he carried Cheryl out, by his face they'd see he wasn't anyone to fear, and his explanation that she'd got drunk and he was taking her home would surely be believed.

*"But she'll be naked, David,"* Mr Clever so rightly pointed out. *"Why would you be carrying a naked woman home?"*

Mr Clever had brought a valid argument to the table, but David had never encountered anyone before, so why would this time be any different?

*"Maybe because you're changing the pattern? There's a first time for everything."*

That unnerved him. Should he take that as a warning?

David thought for a moment, checked his watch—almost one-fifteen in the morning.

Back in the bathroom, he was pleased to see Sally had kept a sharp eye on Cheryl. He took the doll into his bedroom and settled her against the fluffy pillows. One of her eyes blinked, clicking, and he smiled at her.

*Such a good girl.*

Langham was shattered. He'd eaten some of the stale biscuits, but they hadn't filled the gap. He sat at his desk, wishing he could be out looking for Cheryl like Oliver wanted, but his team were working their arses off while he held the fort here. Oliver munched on another packet of crisps, sprawled out as well as anyone could sprawl on an office chair, the grey shadows under his eyes bordering on black.

95

Langham glanced at the wall clock. Well after midnight and time they headed home. He hated to leave, in case something came up, but there was sod all he could do now. Officers had visited the stream and had found nothing. A couple of strategically placed, unmarked cars were positioned on the road at the housing estate, where Langham suspected the killer parked before taking the bodies to the water. They'd remain there throughout the night. Cheryl's parents had been informed—the police in Scotland had been given the grim task of visiting their home and breaking the news. The field was being watched—there was always the possibility the killer would change his pattern and go there, to revisit where he abducted, for no other reason than to be at a place that held importance to him. Every avenue was covered. Cheryl hadn't made contact again, and Oliver hadn't been given any more information dumps. If Cheryl was going to be placed in the stream, they'd catch the fucker before he got the chance to do it. And, if tonight was the night, Langham would be a phone call away should he be needed.

He shouldn't even be here now. Another lead detective, Fairbrother, had arrived fresh-faced and raring to go at shift change, ready to take over where Langham left off, but, like Hastings, Langham hadn't been tired, hadn't wanted to go home. Hastings had finally given in around eleven, saying he'd better get going if he was to be of any use to anyone tomorrow morning.

Yet tomorrow was now, albeit the early hours, and a Saturday at that. Langham had been due a weekend off, but that had gone out of the window as soon as Oliver had turned up with news of Cheryl. It was the nature of the job and something he had to deal with. Didn't mean he had to like it, though.

He sighed and stood. "Come on, you. Home."

Oliver frowned, tossing his empty crisp packet on the desk. It landed near the edge then sailed off, hitting the carpet with a soft crackle. If Langham could be arsed, he'd pick it up, put it in the bin, but he couldn't—and wouldn't.

"Home? But what about—?"

"Nothing we can do tonight now," Langham said. "Until she makes contact or someone calls in that they've spotted him, we may as well take the opportunity to get a bit of shut-eye."

"I doubt I'll sleep. Not until she's found." Oliver got up and scrubbed at his hair, then his face. His stubble rasped against his palms.

"Well, rest then." Langham handed Oliver his jacket. Then he reached for his own. Put it on. "And I'm hungry. The Indian on Blackwater Road will still be open. Closes at two. Fancy a nice korma?"

"I don't want anything."

Langham held back a sigh. "I don't suppose you do. Bloody crisp fiend."

He led the way out of his office and down the stairs. He wouldn't put it past Oliver to have stayed in the office all night, thinking that since Cheryl had contacted him while he'd been there, then that was where she'd be able to get through to him again. But Oliver was often contacted while he was in bed, relaxed, as if him being in that state between awake and asleep was what spirits or people needed in order to reach out and make him hear them.

At the car, Langham clicked it open with his key fob and got into the driver's seat, waiting for Oliver to join him inside. After picking up a couple of curries, some naan bread, and pilau rice at the Indian, he drove home in silence.

"You might as well kip at mine in case we're called out soon," Langham said.

Inside his place, he went into the kitchen to dish up their meals, leaving Oliver to get comfortable on the sofa with a pillow and blanket. When he joined him in the living room with two full plates, he'd expected to find Oliver asleep, completely crashed out, but he was staring at the wall above the TV. Langham stood just inside the doorway and held his breath for a second or two, steam rising off the food and the scents it carried wafting up his nose. He was bloody starving and torn between hoping Oliver was getting something in his head and wanting to at least be able to eat before they had to go out again. Selfish of him to think like that when a woman's life hung in the balance, but if he didn't treat his work as just a job, he'd never have a life of his own. Never have any sane moments.

Oliver didn't have that look he'd had earlier, when he'd been fixated on the office wall, and Langham released his breath.

"Right, food then sleep," he said, sitting in a chair and passing Oliver his plate.

Oliver ate. After a couple of minutes, he said, "We'll find her, won't we?"

"I hope so. But you know the deal, how this kind of thing works—a bit about how the criminal mind works. Sometimes we don't get there in time no matter how hard we try. You know that from the other cases. It's a wanker to accept, but there's nothing we can do about it." Langham gave him an apologetic smile, toying with some sauce-covered rice. "You know me, I won't sugarcoat things. It is what it is." He half shrugged. "I hope we manage it this time, I really do, but if we don't? We tried to save her."

"But sitting here doesn't feel like we're trying to do anything." Oliver stabbed a piece of chicken and put it in his mouth. Chewed slowly, staring down at his plate.

"No, it doesn't, does it, but there are other officers and detectives on it at the moment. You know how we got when we worked Sugar Strands. We kept going through the whole thing, and look how shattered we were afterwards. Remember?"

Oliver swallowed. "But I didn't know the victims then."

"No, there is that. But as far as we're aware, she isn't dead yet. Yes, he's on about taking her home, yes, you said it means death, but it might not mean death right *now*."

He thought of the other women being dumped, their last hours happening close to the weekends, and knew Cheryl was on her way to the end of her life if they didn't find her in time. He refused to remind Oliver of that, though. Best to keep a positive spotlight pointed on things, one that only allowed Oliver to see what that light illuminated, rather than what skulked in the shadows. Shadows had a habit of upsetting him.

"I have to be back at work in a few hours, and I want at least four in kip. Fairbrother can deal with it for now. It's what he's paid for—and he's damn good at his job, too. Nothing like Shields was."

Langham shoved thoughts of Shields away, a detective who'd made it his mission to continually get on Langham's nerves, a man who'd died in the line of duty in the Sugar Strands case. He'd been a prick who'd tormented him and Oliver, and nothing would change that, regardless of whether he was dead or not.

Oliver nodded, and they ate in silence then, save for the ticking of the wall clock and the sound of their forks scraping across their plates.

# CHAPTER NINE

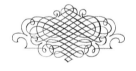

Langham was in the living room chair staring at the ceiling but not seeing it, a throw pulled halfway up his stomach. He'd started falling asleep five minutes ago and couldn't be arsed to break the spell by going to bed. No shaft of moonlight broke through the murkiness as it usually did—the curtains were drawn close together as he hadn't wanted any light in the room at all. No, he wanted blackness, the kind where even if someone lurked in the corner their shadow couldn't be seen. Oliver was on the sofa, breaths the same as when he was awake.

"You want to talk about it?" Langham asked.

"Could do. Might help." Oliver sighed.

"Did you get anything from Cheryl you didn't tell me about? Anything you remember now you're relaxed?"

"I'd hardly call it relaxed."

Oliver would probably do that thing he did, where he closed his eyes and either waited for a new information dump or examined what he'd already been given. Langham imagined that if stuff came at Oliver in a rush, he had to focus on either the voice that shouted the loudest or the imagery that shone the brightest. There was no way, with too much data streaming through his head, he could possibly catch hold of it all. It brought to mind earlier, when Langham had been trying to grasp those snippets, eventually rewarded with the one that had broken free. Was it like that for Oliver?

Langham's need to find Cheryl was somehow stronger, if that were possible, than it had been with the other women. This had got personal now, wasn't just his job when it was a friend of Oliver's they were looking for. So far Cheryl was still alive—or was she? She hadn't spoken to Oliver in a while, so who knew if the man had killed her yet.

He waited, held his breath for a few moments, praying that Oliver got something new. It felt like the air had changed—it had that charged feeling similar to the times in the incident room when everyone was on tenterhooks ready to arrest their man. The hairs on Langham's arms rose as he expelled his breath, and his heart thumped just a bit too hard.

"You all right?" he asked Oliver.

"Yeah, I'm just... There's something...I can't quite get..."

*What's he got? What's he seeing?*

"He's wearing a dark boiler suit."

*Oh fuck, here it is.*

"Like a mechanic," Oliver said, "except he isn't one."

So he'd bought it on purpose? An outfit he used when disposing of the bodies? Was it part of his disguise along with the mask, something he needed to dress up in so he felt...felt what? That he was doing something important, like a job? Did the boiler suit signify just that, a job that he had to get done?

"He's staring at his face in a mirror," Oliver said. "I can see him. See exactly what he looks like."

Langham wanted to get up, switch on the light, and grab a notebook, but he remained in place. Couldn't risk shunting Oliver out of whatever place he was in. But by fuck, it was difficult to stay put.

"Jesus, he's about twenty-two, a little bit older maybe. Doesn't look strong enough to drag women along. Probably why he has to use the drugs. If the women fought, he wouldn't be able to handle them. Puny, he is, more like a teenager than a man. He's got streaky, short blond hair, very green eyes. He has a few faint scars running from his forehead to his temple, spaced apart as though someone…yes, someone has raked their nails down his face at one time—they must have gone pretty deep."

The victims? Had one of the women done that and he'd cleaned all the evidence out from under their nails?

"The scars are old. Years old."

Oh. That put his theory firmly to bed then.

"There's a window behind him, and it's one of those large sheets of glass like flats have."

*High-rise, as we suspected.*

"Outside there's…I can see the clock tower in the city. He's thinking about things being different, but I reckon this has already happened, like, maybe an hour or so ago. I don't feel like I'm seeing it in real time."

"What's different?" Langham winced in case he fucked up Oliver's concentration. *Why don't you just keep your bloody mouth shut?*

"The way he's doing things this time. Cheryl isn't dead. He usually kills them in the bath, holds them under the water, then takes them to the stream. That's why…why all the others have had bleach water in their lungs. Christ Almighty." He paused, then, "No, she isn't dead. He's going to do it at the stream this time."

104

*Thank fuck we have officers out there.*

"That's it. That's all I can get…I'm…"

Langham rang Fairbrother with the new information and told him he'd come back in to work. Fairbrother insisted he shouldn't—everything was under control. Langham didn't take much persuading, there wasn't anything he could do that Fairbrother couldn't. He gave in too easily and resumed his staring at the ceiling.

Why the change now? What had triggered the man into making a new pattern?

Not knowing got to him. He gritted his teeth then closed his eyes, intent on going through everything from the start. He managed up until about three months ago, then his mind seized up on him, a headache blooming at the base of his skull, information scrambling until it made no sense. He fought to clear his head, to go in reverse and continue sifting, but his brain wasn't having any of it. He sighed and allowed the data to drift away, letting in the first signs of sleep—sleep he hadn't thought would come. Darkness converged, slinking into the edges of his vision and obliterated any images that were previously there.

Blank, everything went mercifully blank.

# CHAPTER TEN

Cheryl waited a long time draped over those rocks. She was bloody freezing, her body numb from the cold and the rushing water, but she stayed still, not knowing if he was still there, eyeing her from the bank. She held her breath for as long as she could, until her head lightened and she thought her lungs would burst, and wondered how the fuck she could move without alerting him to the fact that she was still alive.

A swell of water saved her, giving her a chance to naturally lift her head as the rising wet pillow swept past. She turned her head to one side, facing away from the bank, and allowed her cheek to rest on the surface of the icy stream. She remained that way for a while, keeping her breathing shallow and trying to make out any sounds of him watching her. She didn't hear much beyond the gurgle and bubble of the water, the chattering of her teeth, the *whump* of her pulse.

Her arms floated, languid buoys, her fingers stretched into stiff star shapes—from the shock, she reckoned. It seemed as though she had no skin, that the cold rendered her unfeeling, that she was just Cheryl in a shell. Holding her head up took a lot of effort—God, her neck ached—and blackness inched into the edges of her mind, threatening to swallow her up until she passed out. But she held on, told herself she'd get out of this alive if she could.

After a while, she twisted her head the other way, hoping with every faint, slowing beat of her heart that he was gone and she was safe. She forced courage up from deep inside her and opened her eyes. The mud and scrubby grass edge of the bank was closer than she'd expected. Then it hit her. She was too cold to move. *Unable* to move.

*Jesus Christ, no. Please, don't let me die, not when I've come so far…*

With no idea how long she'd stared at the mud and grass, nodules of brown jutting out of water-smoothed earth, sprouts of green that looked black in this light, she shifted her eyes and scanned the rest of the bank. No feet there, no legs or that leering mask. No syringe waiting to jab into her and send her on her final journey—*home-home*, he'd called it. Nothing but dark sky and a moon half covered by deep-grey clouds. She tried lifting herself but failed, so flexed her fingers, determined to get some warmth into her hands and arms, even if just by one degree.

Eventually she moved her arms as though doing the breaststroke, then chanced to draw her hands up the rock beneath her chest and attempt to push herself up on it. She managed a few inches and, with muscles like rubber, smacked back down again, her face plunging into the water. It rushed into her ears, her eyes, and as the force of the splash took over, she listened to a combination of her heartbeat, the whoosh of the water's current, and an odd, quiet humming that brought on the sense that she was doomed, never to get out of the water. Emptiness, a strange void where, for the second it took for her head to make its journey, her chin dashing against the stone, teeth jarring, tongue bitten, death touched her keenly and with eager, grasping hands. No pain, nothing but a dull thud of rock on bone.

She tried again, this time slapping her palm onto the rock and keeping her arm straight for long enough to launch herself sideways. She raised her other arm and clutched at the grass, seeing it, from the meagre light of the moon, inside her curled fingers but not feeling it on her skin. She gripped, she tugged, and hauled herself across, bringing her legs up so she knelt on the rocks. With both hands around clumps of grass, she dragged herself up until she flopped her torso onto the flat of the bank.

Her breaths came in heavy pants, lungs growing sore from the spiteful snap in the air, and she marvelled that even the weather seemed to conspire against her. She laid her head down, resting for a short time to gather her strength, then eased her head up again and dug her elbows into the ground. She army-crawled the rest of the way out of the water then flopped over onto her back, fully expecting to see him looking down at her with those piercing green eyes and that hideous mask.

All she stared at was the murky sky.

She stayed like that for ages, knowing if she didn't get moving soon her body would give up, her organs shutting down on her while she silently screamed for help. She'd close her eyes and just let everything fade away, too weak to fight anymore.

*No. Oliver! Oliver, please, please come and help me.*

A response drifted to her from far away— Oliver's voice, him repeating her name, the chant coming towards her, the chug of a train, closer, closer, closer until it was so loud he could have been standing right beside her.

*"Cheryl? Cheryl? Is that you?"*

*It's me*, she wanted to shout, but the words wouldn't come. Frustrated, she waited to hear more from him, for him to tell her he was on his way and everything would be all right. It took ages for her to raise her hand and manage an awkward rub on her arm, forcing heat into her skin so she'd be able to get the hell out of there. But her body shivered so brutally she couldn't control it, and her hand whipped away from her arm of its own accord, to land on the grass and jolt in vicious jerks.

*"Oliver, please! I'm at the stream. No forest. Just the stream."* She moved her eyes to the side, away from the water. *"A field. It goes on forever."*

She wondered, then, whether it was the field she'd read about, where when you died your loved ones came to collect you in a meadow. But this wasn't the meadow she'd imagined, with bright-green grass highlighted by a beautifully warm sun, with buttercups and daisies swaying in a mild breeze. If this was the field of the hereafter, it was the one belonging to Hell. The one where no one but men like *him* came to collect you.

*"Cheryl? Hang on. We're coming!"*

Those words were too much, too overwhelming, too *needed.* She closed her eyes and bucked from the cold, unable to gain power over the spasms. As everything slipped away, she thought of the sunny meadow and hoped, if Oliver didn't get here in time and she didn't wake up on this plane, she'd open her eyes and see the sun, the daisies and the buttercups. And Gran.

### *Diary Entry #309*

<u>*Quote of the day: Instinct is a valuable thing.*</u>

*No one approached me, and I was able to lay Cheryl in the back seat of my car and strap her in with both seat belts. The drive to my usual street by the stream didn't take long, but I didn't park there. I had this dodgy feeling in my gut and decided to stop somewhere else—that someone was watching. The hairs on the back of my neck stood up, and I got goosebumps that matched Cheryl's. So I went down this side street then turned off onto a track. Left the car behind some bushes and carried her as far as I could away from Morrisons. And I mean way away. Farther than I've been before. It took a while, what with having to trek through the forest first, and a few times her hair snagged on tree trunks and low branches.*

*By the time I'd left the forest and tramped over some fields, got to what I felt was a safe part of the stream, I was knackered. Panting. My arms ached— she'd grown heavier than when I'd lifted her off the bed before her bath—and I wondered if she'd snuffed it, but it was just my muscles aching from carrying her so far.*

*I kept walking until I found some rocks like the ones I'd chosen before and placed her over them, belly down. She looked like a hill, a stark, white hill in the darkness. I put her face in the water then clicked the light on my watch so I could watch a full minute tick by. I'd planned to wait longer, to make sure she drowned—five minutes or more—but something rustled in the field behind me, and I shit myself.*

*Mr Clever told me to get going, go home, so I left.*

*Instead of going straight home, I visited The Stick after. That place is so weird, all rusty oil drums and bummed-out people with greasy hair and dirty clothes.*

*I can't wait to see Conrad tomorrow. Well, it's later today, isn't it. Time to get a bit of kip. We usually meet about nine o'clock. I'll clean my place when I come back home after breakfast.*

*I won't be going in to work. Too tired.*

# CHAPTER ELEVEN

With blankets tossed over his shoulder, Langham sprinted out of the forest and into a field, heading towards the oval of illumination provided by the spotlight from the helicopter circling above. Its heat-seeking equipment had found Cheryl perilously close to the stream, and he was fucked if he'd get there too late. Oliver kept pace with him, and the air from the rotors blew back Langham's hair, rippled his cheeks, and his eyes dried out. The grass flattened, spreading out into a crop circle. A black-clad figure dangled from a rope ladder, getting lower by the second. He reached the ground then ran to the stream bank. Langham and Oliver arrived there seconds later, getting the nod from the man in black that yes, she was alive, and yes, they needed to get her the fuck out of there.

Oliver draped the foil blanket he'd brought with him over her and knelt to tuck it under her so she was encased. Langham added the other blankets then tapped Oliver on the shoulder and motioned for him to get up and out of the way. Pointless speaking—the helicopter was too loud. They stepped back, allowing room for two more men from the chopper bearing a stretcher. Cheryl was gently lifted onto it, and the men carried her away. The chopper had landed, and Cheryl was settled on board. Then the great metal bird lifted and tilted a little to one side, shooting off.

Langham looked at Oliver, the *whap-whap-whap* of the helicopter distant now. "We got her."

Oliver blinked.

There was nothing more to say, so they walked back to the forest, heads bent, hands in pockets, Langham wondering how the hell that woman had survived. She was unconscious, from the cold, drugs, and exhaustion, he imagined, but so long as her body didn't go into shock and break down on her, she'd likely come through this okay. But what

116

of her mind? What about the mental scars? He dreaded to think what she'd have to face when she woke up, and again once she drifted back to sleep, the nightmares coming, treating her without mercy, relentless in their quest to fracture her further.

Branches grabbed at his trousers, but he didn't give a shit. He yanked his legs away and kept going, other officers coming into view ahead, torchlight bobbing erratically as they ran. There was still so much to do.

They turned once the officers had come closer, back the other way to lead the men to where Cheryl had been found. As they all stood on the bank a metre or so from the spot, Langham explained her position, how he'd found her. Officers spoke into radios while others gazed around, probably working out which direction the killer had come from and what had possessed him to bring her out this far. Why had he changed where he'd left her? Why so far from the others?

*Did he go to do his usual thing and spot the undercover policemen in those cars? Did he realise they were there? Could the officers have seen him drive past and not even have known it?*

He stared at the rocks poking out of the water and shook his head. What the hell *was* it about them? Why did the killer put the women into position over them? It had to be significant, and when he caught the fucker, that would be one of the first questions he asked.

It took half an hour of waiting around before SOCO and Detective Fairbrother arrived to take over. Langham and Oliver left the scene, traipsing back through the forest to where he'd parked his car haphazardly, half on the uneven track, half off. Squad cars dotted the way out, their occupants preparing to leave the vehicles and join those on the stream bank. Once they were in his car, Langham whacked up the heat, cold to the bone and thinking he had no clue what cold really was compared to Cheryl. As he drove through the city, he wondered whether Cheryl was warm yet, whether she was getting some feeling back into her, because fuck, she'd had to have been freezing in that water.

He glanced at the clock on the dash, the luminous green numbers glowing five-fifteen. He pondered on whether to go home for a couple of hours, but it was pointless. He was wide awake, and Oliver was sitting beside him, anxious, Langham reckoned, to see Cheryl.

"Hospital?" Langham glanced across at him.

Oliver nodded. "Yeah. I'll wait with her until her parents get there. She's got no one else."

# CHAPTER TWELVE

David was meant to be at work, but he rang in sick. He was too tired, the amount of restless sleep he'd had fucking with his equilibrium. He didn't like feeling so out of sorts. It reminded him of being a kid. Not knowing what was around the corner. Well, that wasn't strictly true. As a child he'd always known what had lurked at the bend on Don't Hurt Me Avenue, just not when the bogeywoman, his mother, would make an especially nasty appearance. And she *was* nasty.

He studied Conrad across the table in Morrisons, their breakfast plates piled with a full English, their tea brewing in the pot. Conrad was a right bloody mess. Looked like he hadn't slept very well either.

David cursed himself for not asking Cheryl about the availability of tea cosies.

Conrad was bursting with shit to tell him— obvious, it was—so David raised his eyebrows as a signal for the prick to start talking while David tucked into his breakfast. He needed Conrad now—more so than he had in the past. Before, the man had been a semblance of a friend, something David hadn't had before. He could fool himself into thinking he was liked, that if he chose to, he could go out with Conrad on the lash and eye up the girls. But Conrad had never asked him—maybe he would one day—and girls had never appealed to David in that way. They reminded him too much of the bogeywoman.

"I went to the newspaper, like you suggested," Conrad said, "and she hasn't been there either."

David swallowed a piece of fried egg. And the knot of emotion in his throat. He needed to get focused, to concentrate on the here and now. "Look, how long has it been again?" He flapped his fork midair, feigning casual when inside he felt that *thing* creeping back, that desperately depressing thing that, once it took hold, was a bastard to shake off. "You know what? Time doesn't matter at this stage. Some people, if they've got problems, just take off for a bit. No explanation, nothing. They have so much going on in their head that it's best to stay away. Or they go off into a world of their own, a different world to this one, where they can be someone else and not worry about shit." He was dangerously close to letting something slip.

*"Be quiet, David,"* Mr Clever said.

"Didn't I tell you this before?" David asked. "About people just taking off? That's why the police don't usually follow up on an adult missing person until they've been gone more than forty-eight hours. People just need a breather, a break. Two or three days, and I bet she turns up."

David worked hard to stop himself smiling. Someone would stumble upon her—not a dog-walker this time. No, it might be the farmer or maybe one of the people who worked for him. Off out in the fields thinking they had a normal day's work ahead of them and, 'Oh, what the hell's that in the stream there? Good fucking Lord, it's a body!'

"She'll reappear, and everyone'll wonder where she's been, what she's been doing and who with, but I reckon she won't tell anyone a thing," David said.

"How come you think she won't say anything?" Conrad frowned. "She owes her bosses an explanation, at least. Me, even. You don't just not arrive for a date or work, do you?" Conrad looked at him funny, like he knew something David didn't. Like he was trying to draw something out of him.

*"Watch him, David. He might cause you trouble, and we wouldn't want that, would we..."*

"Oh, come on! Lots of people do." David cut a bacon rasher in half. "Bet if you plugged it into Google, you'd see a shitload of links about people who've been stood up with no explanation."

"Yeah, but—"

"Jesus, Conrad. Will you listen to yourself? Anyone would think you were a couple or something, like she should have told you where she's gone, but bloody hell, she just knows you as some bloke she serves breakfast to. Sorry to be blunt, but that's the way it is. Sounds to me like all the strong feelings are on your side anyway, so yeah, you *would* be expecting her to care and let you know where she's gone. But look at it from her point of view. Let's just say she doesn't dig you as much as you dig her. You're not important, she doesn't *care* about you, so therefore, when she decided to take off or whatever the fuck she did, I bet you didn't even figure in her thoughts." *That should shut him up.*

"Her neighbours haven't heard her dog barking like it usually does." Conrad gave a self-satisfied smile. "What do you think about *that?*"

David stared at him. Conrad had gone so far as to visit her house and speak to the fucking *neighbours?* "You *asked* them?"

"Yeah, I asked them. Someone's got to give a shit."

David shook his head and sighed as though he was weary of Conrad's worrying ways. The child in him reared up. No, he was a man now. Everything would be okay. *Don't take me back there. Don't hurt me.* "You're persistent, I'll give you that much. Not sure I'd be the same in your position."

He had to find out more. Had to stop his mind splitting in three first, though. One piece wanted to be David, the other wanted to be that man who took girls and did that weird shit, and the last, his kid self.

*Come on. Concentrate. Conrad might prove to be a pain in the arse if he pokes around asking any more questions.*

"So tell me," David said, "did you actually find anything out that would be useful to the police? They're not going to listen to you with what you've got, you know."

Conrad speared a sausage then bit off the end. He seemed to chew forever. "Well, that's where you're wrong. From what I gathered, she was seen leaving her house that night with her dog. The night she was supposed to meet me. Seven-thirty on the dot, as always. She headed for the field just over there, and someone else walking their dog saw her but couldn't remember the exact time. Estimate is just before eight, he said."

"You *spoke* to someone where she walks her *dog?*" David had failed to hide his surprise and kicked himself under the table.

"You okay?"

"Yeah. Got cramp. Carry on."

*"That was a good one, David. You're getting very adept at thinking on your feet. It won't be long, and you may well be able to do this sort of thing without my help. Would you like going it alone?"*

"Yeah, some bloke who comes in here," Conrad said. "I nipped in yesterday afternoon once I remembered earwigging to a conversation she'd had with him. They'd talked about seeing one another while walking their dogs once. He comes in at two every day. You know the one? Bald with a penny-sized birthmark on his neck. Well…" Conrad played with his food. "I got this idea after I spoke to him. You know I said about those women?"

David's head spun. "What women?"

"The ones The Weirdo is taking. God, we talked about this!"

*"Keep calm, David,"* Mr Clever said. *"Even if he says what you think he's going to say, keep calm."*

"Yeah," David said, relieved he'd sounded normal.

"I looked up some stuff online about The Weirdo, and the last couple of women he took, he only kept them for about two days each."

*Fuck.*

"And?" David's heart rate increased. He didn't like it. *Don't hurt me.*

"And so I went to the stream last night."

"You did *what?*" It had burst out before David had been able stop it.

"I know!" Conrad beamed. "Good idea, eh?"

"Are you nuts? That bloke is dangerous."

*"He isn't, David. Not yet."*

Conrad's nose twitched. "I found a dead dog. Stank, it did. Some bastard had sliced up its belly. Who would *do* something like that, eh?"

David didn't know what to say. It felt like the contents of his body had seeped out and left him hollow. Like that dog. He stared at Conrad for a moment, gripping his knife and fork. Mr Clever hissed, giving him the nudge he needed to act normal. "You told the police about this? You didn't just leave the dog there, did you?"

"Yep, told the police."

"Where did you find it?"

"This end of the stream, where the bald bloke said he'd last seen her."

David went cold. He wondered whether Cheryl was as cold. Whether, if he went back and touched her, she'd freeze his fingers. Whether she'd understand from where she was in *home-home*, why he'd chosen her. Maybe he ought to do that next time. Tell them why they were there—but he didn't know why himself.

*"Yes, you do, David."*

"What time was that?" Why hadn't Mr Clever warned him about Conrad before now? Why had he let them meet and make David think he could have a friend, only to have that friend taken away when something like this happened? He'd never abducted a man before, had never felt the need, but he might have to do that now. Snatch Conrad and make him go *home-home*.

David's head felt like it was going to burst. There was too much information inside it, things from back then and things from now, all vying for his immediate attention. And he couldn't cope with both parts of himself, not at the same time. It sent him doolally.

"About eight. I didn't get home until after midnight, though. They wanted a statement, the police, and I swear they thought I had something to do with it at first. This detective asked questions about what I'd been doing, and I thought it was to trip me up, get me to admit something I hadn't done—admit to being *him*." Conrad shuddered. "Like anyone would want to be him. That man's sick in the head."

*I don't like you saying that.*

"But in the end, they didn't," Conrad said. "Think it was me, I mean."

"How come? What changed their mind?"

"That copper, Langham, he spoke to me. His associate got information—that psychic shit he does—that proves I'm not involved."

"What kind of information?" David hoped he'd just sounded interested, your average nosy parker.

Conrad shifted in his seat as though excited. "He didn't say, probably confidential, but the rozzers who spoke to me after him *did* say if The Weirdo has Cheryl, they'll find her—and him."

David was having a dream but couldn't pull himself out of it. It was one of those odd ones where you were conscious of reality yet the world in which you currently stood seemed just as real,

126

just as vivid. He was in the living room of his childhood home, the velvet sofa opposite against the back wall, his mother sitting on it, staring at him with those muddy-brown eyes of hers. He was trapped, rooted to the spot by her unwavering glare.

*What have I done now? Why am I here? I haven't been here for ages, since I started meeting the women. Everything was okay. What's happened to make it different?*

"Why couldn't you have been a girl, David?" the bogeywoman asked.

*Not that. Please, not that...*

"Why couldn't I have had my little corn-blonde, green-eyed princess?"

She had her legs crossed, one perfect, slim pin dangling over the other. She bounced the top one, the flesh of her calf barely spreading as it met the shin below. Her bleached hair was that corn colour she so wanted David to have. His father's black had diluted her original brunette, producing a shade on their child that made him an inbetweener—something that didn't fit into either category. Rather like himself. He was in-between everywhere, a boy who wanted to be a girl but with no real desire or gene to allow him to be female. He was a boy, with boy things on his mind—climbing trees, playing marbles in the dirt, kicking a football about—yet he'd been given that doll for his fifth birthday and was expected to wear dresses when he was at home.

*There's something wrong with that, I know it, but I can't tell her, can't explain it to her because everything's just so messy, so fuzzy. And she wouldn't understand.*

"I don't know," he said, his usual, standard answer. He clenched his little boy fists at his sides, staring back at her with an adult mind in a child's body.

"You never know anything much, David. If you'd have been a girl you'd have known so much more. Girls are so *clever*."

*No, they're not. If they were, they wouldn't get taken. I wouldn't be able to do what I've done. I proved it, didn't I? Proved that boys are cleverer?*

He'd best not to say anything in response to her statement. If he argued, she'd win. She always had in the past, so why would her being in his dream be any different?

"Where's Sally, David?" she went on without waiting for him to answer. "That's what I would have called you if you'd been a girl."

He inwardly shrugged—couldn't do it outright because she'd smack him for it. Smacks hurt, didn't they? His skin was always so sore afterwards, on fire, the site of her strike a handprint of heat. Sometimes he couldn't sit, had to lean over onto his other arse cheek, his underpants chafing over it—God, it brought tears to his eyes every time.

He resisted shrugging again. She didn't like shruggers. His father did it a lot, and it drove her mad, she said—or shouted, depending on her mood. She smacked Dad sometimes, too, right across the face, and once her sharp fingernails had brushed his father's eyeball and he'd had trouble seeing properly for weeks. David understood the pain of that. Those fingernails regularly bit into the soft skin of his underarm, or on his face as she dragged him along, heading for the stairs and his room where she'd do more than smack him with her hand. She'd kick him, too.

"You need to take good care of that dolly, David. She cost a lot of money."

Mother smiled, lips free of colour, eyelids and cheeks the same. She didn't wear makeup—didn't need it she was so beautiful. Yet she was ugly to him, her perfect features nothing but horrendous to look at. Dad said she hadn't always been like this, that she'd changed when David had been born. And David wasn't to take that to heart, all right? It wasn't his fault, it was his mother's. And as much as Dad had tried to stand up to her on his behalf, most of the time Dad had just sat back and let it all happen because he could never win. Never.

The Sally in the Fire incident was a time when David…when he'd become well and truly lost. His father, as an anchor, had been cruelly taken away.

"I'm not letting him have that doll anymore, Lisabeth! He's a damn boy, not a bloody girl. Get over it!"

Sally had sailed from Dad's hand and into the fire, her round-eyed gaze changing to narrow as her eyelids had closed, melting. David had lunged forward, knowing he had to take good care of Sally like his mother had told him. Knowing if he didn't save her, he'd have no one left—no one to cuddle at night or talk to if things got too bad—and Mother would belt him for not looking after Sally even though it was his father who had thrown her there.

"You fucking bastard." Mother had glided across the room much like Sally had, launching into Dad and knocking him onto the sofa, flapping her hands, raining those evil smacks down on him.

David had burnt his hand getting his dolly out, but rolled Sally until the flames went away, and blew on her cheeks until the plastic cooled and she didn't look so squidgy anymore.

Mother had smacked on until Dad hadn't move any longer, and she'd said something about a heart attack.

Now, Mother brought David out of his reverie with a sharp clearing of her throat. He blinked to rid himself of the images in his mind, to dissolve the film of tears.

"You're a little bastard, David, and I'm tired of you now. Go away."

The room faded around him, but the hurt didn't. It flared brighter than it had before, always did, the pain becoming more intense every time he saw her in his dreams. She lived in his head, inside his body, still directing everything he did and said, although he did a good job of shutting her out these days. Or had, until now.

As he walked backwards out of that living room, the pull of consciousness tugging at his back like he tugged Sally's musical cord, he thought about the newspaper and whether Cheryl's discovery would get better coverage. If it did, at least someone was taking more notice. At least someone cared enough about him to tell the country a little of what he'd done. At least he'd be known as being clever.

# CHAPTER THIRTEEN

Langham looked around the packed incident room. The night shift had stayed on for the meeting—easier to bring everyone up to date that way—and Oliver was at work at the newspaper. Those who had gone home yesterday and returned this morning appeared refreshed and ready to go. Their schedules would be busy, and what Langham had in mind meant the majority of them might need to do overtime. He'd possibly need a double team to make this go off without a hitch.

Detective Fairbrother was currently going through everything that had happened overnight for the benefit of those not in the know. Langham had been through it with him already, so he centred his thoughts on what was to come tonight.

It pained him to have to do something Villier had suggested—using her as bait—but if they were going to catch this man, they needed to orchestrate things so he did what Langham wanted, when he wanted.

He'd been thinking about profiles earlier that morning. Many serial killers admitted after being caught that they'd enjoyed reading about what they'd done in the newspapers. Now might be the time to try to rile the killer with a paragraph designed to make their man act out of character, change his pattern. A snippet of coverage on Cheryl was in order. He had a press conference scheduled a bit later, and after this meeting he'd go and write down exactly what he wanted the killer to know.

Villier wasn't aware he was going to be taking her up on her offer. He'd soon see if she was all mouth and no trousers.

"Right then," he said when Fairbrother had finished. "It goes without saying that we're keeping Miss Witherspoon's situation under wraps. The information stays in here." He swept an arm out to encompass the room. "And in here." He tapped his temple. "Anyone found to have a loose mouth at this stage in the game will be severely reprimanded. It is *crucial* we stick to what myself and Detective Fairbrother discussed in my office earlier this morning—I'll be going over that with you in a second. No one talks to the press, understand? No one. If you're caught slipping out any information, just be aware you won't be working on my team in the future, possibly reduced to mundane tasks downstairs. Like cleaning pissed-up prisoners' puke. Maybe even losing your job altogether. You getting the idea?"

Everyone murmured agreement.

"It's a privilege to be on this team, not something you're entitled to, so remember that if you're approached by reporters or your other halves at home try to get you to talk about it. No one's indispensable—everyone's easily replaced. This isn't the same case as it was before. We had no clues and it was cold, but now it's hot as fuck, and we need to work hard to make sure it doesn't get any hotter. Which brings me to what we're doing today and tonight. Day shift, you might want to ring home and let your people know you'll be doing overtime, just in case we need you. Anyone who seriously can't needs to let me know now so Detective Fairbrother can rearrange who is doing what."

He paused, looking at everyone in turn. No one raised a hand. No one sighed in frustration. Each

135

face showed how determined they all were to see an end to this, to wrap it up and put it to bed.

"Good. I'll thank you now for your dedication because I won't have time to do it until this is all over."

He glanced at Villier, who stared back with an expression showing her steely fortitude to be a major player in this case. She'd make a formidable detective, but he was fucked if she'd be on his team, his shift. If she made the grade, he'd put in a quiet suggestion to the chief that they worked on opposite teams, different hours. The least he saw of her the better. She wound him up.

"Sergeant Villier suggested about being used as bait," he said.

He peeked at her to see if she appeared smug or shocked. As he'd suspected, smug. She knew damn well what was coming and would use it to her advantage at the next detective opening that her suggestion had been integral to this investigation—that it had secured the killer's arrest. Still, there was no time to get pissed off about how she'd act in the future—more smugness, more 'I told you so'—because they had limited hours and a lot to get sorted.

"We'll be taking her up on that offer—with a wig and contacts—using a K9 for authenticity. What the killer won't know is that the dog is trained to attack with a simple click of the fingers and a one-word command. Any clue at all he's our man, and he'll be taken down." He looked at Villier. "You'll be wired, we'll be listening. You'll be watched, we'll be in various locations—outside Morrisons in vehicles, in the forest. At no time will you be out of sight or earshot, understand?"

She crossed her arms over her chest, crinkling her crisp white shirt, her tie curving into a capital C.

"You'll need to come to my office to discuss the finer details later. Detective Fairbrother will be going home shortly for a quick nap then returning, but those others on the night shift only need to come in two hours earlier than usual. I'll go over exactly where everyone needs to be in a moment, using this map here"—he pointed to one attached to a whiteboard—"and then those who are due to go home, go home. Those who need to stay will help with the setup process."

It took an hour to go over everything, and he felt sorry for those officers who were flagging, but there wasn't anything he could do about it. This fucker needed catching, and if they could draw him out tonight, all the better, but they'd send Villier out as bait every night until they caught him. A huge amount of man hours and power—and he doubted the budget would cover it—but he had no choice now. Money would have to take a back seat on this one since they were so close to catching him.

With everyone off doing their assigned jobs, Langham walked through the main office and jerked his head at Villier, who followed him into the small kitchen. She leant her arse against the worktop and rested one arm beneath her breasts.

She chewed at a thumbnail. Langham pretended he hadn't noticed and put the kettle on, afterwards spooning coffee then sugar into two cups.

She cleared her throat. "I know I come off as a pretentious bitch but—"

"It's okay, I get it." He still didn't look at her. Grabbed a cloth off the sink and wiped the sides instead.

"You do?"

He nodded. "Yep, woman copper in a male-dominated world. I know. I understand. Might not like the way you are, but I get it." He watched her from the corner of his eye.

She fiddled with her long fringe, winding it around her finger. "I don't mean to come off like that, it just happens. I get this thing inside me that won't allow for any softness." She laughed quietly. "Probably afraid that if I do, someone will take advantage or won't listen to my orders because I'm female."

The kettle boiled, and the switch snapped up.

Langham poured water into the cups, set about adding milk. "You're a sergeant. People ought to do as they're told because of that, not because you don't have a dick, pardon my bluntness."

"I prefer blunt."

"I'd gathered that."

He smiled at her then, and she smiled back, a proper grin, one with teeth and gums. She reached for the coffee he handed her, then he jerked his head again, walking without speaking until they went into his office and closed the door. He

138

gestured for her to take a seat and sat in his chair, glad he'd cleared away the biscuits from yesterday, had got rid of the crumbs and that bloody fluff in the gouge. She'd have frowned at that had it still been there.

"So you're frightened," he said. She liked blunt, she'd get it. "I understand that, too. And I also understand that it's normal for you to feel this way even though it was your suggestion that you be used as bait. But, like I said back there, you'll be monitored. From what Cheryl told Fairbrother during the night, he jabbed her with the needle then killed her dog before she lost consciousness. It won't even get that far with our operation. It'll be obvious who he is as soon as he approaches. We'll give it about two hours, in case he's watching. Lots of people take their dogs out for that amount of time. Any more, though, and we're pushing it. He'll know something's up if he's there somewhere, taking note of your movements."

"What if he's not there tonight?" She sipped her coffee. Her hand trembled a bit.

"Then we'll return tomorrow evening. You'll walk and play with the dog; the killer will hopefully think you're new to the area or whatever. Doesn't matter what he thinks on that score—so long as it looks normal, authentic, it'll work. If you keep glancing at the road, Morrisons, or the forest, he might get suspicious. Many people walk with their heads down. They take a bit of time to have a think while their dog ferrets about on its own. Do that. We can let you know when someone's approaching. Your earpiece is a bud—he won't notice it if we use a long wig."

She took it all in, probably visualising it in her mind. She stared at the floor, finger still twirling that hair. "So if he approaches, what do I say? Is there anything you *want* me to say?"

"No. Take it as it comes. Respond as you would if this wasn't a setup and you were out and about and someone came along to chat you up." He wondered how many men *had* chatted her up and if they'd received a sharp refusal. Then again, she might not be an uptight bitch all the time.

"Right." She let out a long, unsteady breath. "Right."

She was mentally convincing herself she could do this, he knew that. He'd be doing the same in her position. And it wasn't like she had much time to get used to it either. No going home to sleep on it. She'd have a few hours then be dumped into the path of a madman.

It must have taken courage for her to open up to him like this, reveal the chink in her armour. She'd never struck him as the confiding type, so he supposed he ought to feel pleased she'd chosen him. He wasn't. Didn't give a fuck how she felt. Her attitude had always rubbed him up the wrong way, so the shutters had come down where she was concerned. He'd keep her vulnerability to himself, though, as much as he was tempted to be an arsehole and tell someone she wasn't such a hard cow after all. It wouldn't do for anyone else to know she actually had a heart, was human, because, like she'd said, it meant they might not take her seriously. And, if she was thinking of becoming a detective, she'd need to retain her icy veneer.

"So, have you got anything dog-walkerish to wear?" he asked.

"Not here, no."

He leant forward, pulling his wallet out of his back trouser pocket. Selecting two tenners, he handed them over. "Go out and buy something. Cheap joggers and a sweatshirt or something—there's nothing like that in the spare clothes cupboard. Keep the receipts." He took out another twenty. "Best get some training shoes as well."

"What, training shoes for twenty quid?" she said, putting the money in her shirt pocket.

"We're not talking Nikes, Villier." He held back a smile. "Like I said, something cheap."

"What if he's a brand-name snob?" She raised her eyebrows.

"He isn't."

"How do you know?"

"Oliver sensed it with one of his info dump episodes. Casual dresser."

"Oh. Right. So that's that then. Oliver has spoken." She stood and walked over to the door.

He slid his wallet into his pocket, thinking that he'd let her snarky comment about Oliver slide, but if she did it again, he'd fucking give her what for.

He sat in silence after she'd left, drank his coffee, emptying his mind and just enjoying the taste, the silence. Before long he'd be running around like a blue-arsed fly, no time to stop. He lifted the phone and dialled Oliver's mobile.

"You coming to the press conference in a bit?" Langham asked.

"Yeah. I just got back from visiting Cheryl. Her parents are here. They looked knackered. Drove down through the night."

"How is she?"

"Awake. Tearful."

Langham nodded. "I think I'll send Villier to see her this afternoon. Might help her for tonight."

"What's going on tonight?"

"Won't say much until I see you, but she's going out with a dog."

"Christ."

"It's got to be done. Can't let this go on the way it has been. If he gets another one…"

"But what if she doesn't stand out to him? What if he picks someone else?"

"Then we'll still be there, watching."

"But for how long? He might take a break like he's done in the past."

"I don't think he will after he sees what'll be in the second edition of today's paper."

"Ah."

"Listen, I'm going to have to go," Langham said.

"I want to be there tonight."

"Oliver, I don't think—"

"I'll keep out of it, stay out of the way. I want to see him get caught."

"I understand. Right then. I'm off. Lots on. Careful with that kettle at work now. All those teas…"

"Fuck off."

Langham ended the call, chuckling. The smile was wiped off his face, though, when he thought about all those women before Cheryl, what they'd been through. He had no idea what that was until Cheryl told them exactly what had happened to her.

He thought of The Stick and how he didn't recall anyone updating him on a visit there. He frowned and stood, suddenly pissed off with himself for not asking at the meeting, annoyed at Fairbrother for not mentioning it in his summing up. Or had Langham just not heard that bit? He left his office, heading for the main room with thunder in his thoughts—just in case someone needed a bollocking.

# CHAPTER FOURTEEN

D avid needed to force himself out of bed before depression got a hold on him. If he wasn't careful, he'd slip back to how he used to be—a mess of uncertainty, the past swirling around in his head, none of it going down the drain because he couldn't seem to pull the plug. But he'd managed it, hadn't he? Focusing on the women meant he'd had other things to think about, and his past had faded away, only remaining on the peripheral of his mind. Cheryl had done something to him, though. He thought it might have been her saying he didn't get on her nerves or whatever. She hadn't said what the bogeywoman had always said. Or was it him leaving her at her final resting place that had been wrong? He'd made a mistake somewhere but couldn't think what it was. That bad dream about his mother had muddled him up.

He couldn't think now. Was better off just getting up, having a shower. The water would help clear the fog, and maybe he'd find where he'd fucked up—if he even had. See, that was what those dreams did to him—he second-guessed himself.

Under the water, each stream needle-like when it hit his skin, he thought over Cheryl's transportation and delivery. Knew exactly what the problem was then. He hadn't waited long enough, hadn't checked that she'd actually drowned. But that rustle behind him, maybe of an animal, had... No, it hadn't frightened him, it *hadn't.*

*"It did. Stop lying to yourself."*

"What should I do?" David turned the water off and reached for a towel. He stood on the bathmat, shivering despite the terry cloth swaddling him, and stared at his reflection in the mirror above the sink, seeing remnants of his dream in his mind and blatant fear in his eyes. Where had his self-confidence gone? It was Conrad's fault. He'd started it—the insecurity, the questions. And his last comment, the one about that copper finding The Weirdo. Shit. That wouldn't be very nice.

*"It's coming on for four o'clock. Second edition of the paper should be out by now. You ought to get dressed, go out for a walk, pick up a copy."*

"Yeah." He nodded. "Yeah, I'll do that."

He dressed hurriedly then glanced around his flat—he should clean but wanted to read the paper more. Would she even have been found yet, so far out as she was? He didn't think so, didn't reckon she'd be noticed for weeks.

Out on his street, he shoved his hands in his jacket pockets and walked to the corner, glancing right and left, crossing the road and heading towards the little newsagents down the way a bit. The bloke behind the counter got on his nerves— nosy bastard, he was—and always asked what David had been up to, as though he *knew.* He stared at him oddly, too, his head tilted and a look in his eye that seemed to snake right under David's skin.

"Fucking prick," he said and entered the shop.

He walked straight to the paper stand, pleased a stack of second editions sat on the floor beside it but annoyed they still had the crisscross of tape over them where no one had bought a copy. If she'd been found and her story was on the front page and no one had seen it, what was the point in doing what he'd done? He took his keys out of his pocket, selected his penknife on the ring, and cut the tape. It sprang back, and he stared at the front page. He'd made the lower half again—*only the lower fucking half*—and he resisted the urge to kick that sodding paper pile and punch the shop owner in the face.

Instead, he calmly lifted a copy then strolled over to the counter.

"Nasty business, that," the shop owner said, nodding sagely. "You'd think they'd have caught the bastard who's doing it by now, wouldn't you. I mean, he's done it often enough for them to have found some sort of evidence, surely."

David drew some change from his pocket and handed over a quid. Waited for the man to ring it up and give him his change.

*Come on, tosser, hurry up.*

"Got to be a right strange sort to do something like that, haven't you," Tosser said.

David shrugged. *Don't hurt me. I didn't mean to shrug.*

"Who in their right mind would go about killing women, though, eh?" Tosser jabbed one porky finger at a button on his till. He paused. "Got to be a nutter." He shook his head. "Got to be."

David didn't want to fully take in what he'd said—*nutter, nutter, nutter*—so blinked a few times and concentrated on the packets of mints on the shelf behind Tosser. He inhaled deeply, a big fuck-off suck of air, then blew it out, his breath raising one corner of the front page of his newspaper. Tosser finally finished ringing the sale up and gave David his change. David stared down at it, the money glinting from the strip lights above, then he thrust it in his pocket and picked up his paper. Left the shop while Tosser prattled on, knowing he'd be called all the names under the cloud-covered sun once the door closed after him.

He raced back to his flat. He never read the paper while he walked, preferring to browse it in the comfort of his own home, scanning the articles at rapid-fire speed the first time then slowing on the subsequent go through, savouring everything, reading between the lines—around the lines, behind the fucking lines—to see if there was some hidden message there. There never was. Just straight reporting. Boring reporting.

Home. He didn't bother taking off his coat. He sat on his bed and positioned Sally next to him so she could see, too. He smoothed the paper on his knees and took in the size of the article. Full bottom half. The headline was larger than before, all in black caps.


## ANOTHER VICTIM, ANOTHER ISLAND IN THE STREAM

They'd found her? Already? Jesus Christ!

He read fast, the words seeming to tumble over one another on the page, dancing, running away from where they were supposed to be and stopping somewhere else. He closed his eyes, took a deep breath, then opened them again to read at a slower pace.

*Another body was found in the early hours of this morning by a farmer looking for one of his stray cows. Cheryl Witherspoon had been missing for two days, and it is estimated she was left at the stream—farther up from the other victims—between one and two a.m.*

How did they know that? How did they always get it right?

*As with the other victims, Miss Witherspoon had not been subjected to sexual abuse. However, she was drugged, but, unlike the others, she wasn't killed before she was placed in the water.*

*Detective Langham, lead officer on this case, said, "I don't feel the man responsible will have enough courage to approach another woman in the near future. From what we've seen, he needs time to recover between abductions, almost as though he's weakened from dealing with what he's done. A weak man, very weak."*

Why had Langham repeated himself? David wasn't weak. No fucking way was he.

He clenched his teeth and read on.

*"I suggest remaining vigilant, especially if you're a female dog walker, but I wouldn't change your day-to-day life. The man we're looking for, despite coming across as frightening due to abducting women then killing them, is actually a weak-willed*

*individual who possibly suffers from an inferiority complex."*

There it was again. Weak.
Bastard.

*"Profilers have suggested he's been made to feel useless in the past, therefore, him taking women is a form of control, something he can use to make himself feel better. What we'll also probably discover when he's caught—and he will be—is the fact that he lacks guts. He possibly thinks he's brave, but I believe he's far from it. If he was brave, he'd take another woman tonight, wouldn't he, to prove me wrong."*

David's face burned. Reading about himself like that was more than a little disturbing. How did they know so much just from the bodies and where he'd put them, when he'd taken them? How did his personality come into it? He rubbed his temple, unable to understand where they'd got their information from—it was so accurate, too. He *did* need time between selecting women. He *had* been weak-willed in the past, *did* have an inferiority complex, but what they *didn't* know, the cocky bastards, was he was none of those things now. The women had seen to that.

"What do you think, Sally?" he whispered. "Shall I show them I'm brave? That I have the courage to bring another friend home tonight?"

He glanced at her, and his movement jostled the mattress, sending Sally sprawling backwards, her stiff legs sticking up in the air. Her dress lifted, exposing her naked, private garden, and he hurriedly covered her up, pleased she didn't have that messy redness like the women did. Her eyelid clicked as it opened and closed. He sat her on his lap, her feet beneath the newspaper, and let her read the article for herself.

"You agree, don't you, Sally?"

He thought she nodded, thought she gave him the thumbs-up, and that was good enough for him. A glance at his alarm clock on the bedside cabinet told him he had just enough time to clean before going out and making friends with another woman and her dog.

He polished and bleached, hoovered then mopped, and thought about how all those women looked like Mother after he'd bleached them. They changed right before his eyes from the minute he took them to the second he laid them in the stream water, and that was what Mother had done, hadn't she? After Dad hadn't woken up on the night of the Sally in the Fire Incident, Mother had become worse. After Dad had been taken away, Mother muttering about the cost of a funeral and how she'd been left with her useless prick of a son, she'd got worse.

Still, David had put *her* in the stream in the end. Sixteen years old, he'd been, but he'd managed it well enough. She'd tried to speak to him when he'd bleached her—his way of trying to remove the badness in her, on her, to make her clean so she'd be the nice woman she'd once been—but the medicine had slurred her words. He hadn't intended to kill her. Not until she'd managed to speak coherently after he'd spent some time sanitising every part of her.

"You fucking piece of shit, David." Her words had been slow, dragged out. "I hate you. Have always hated you. You...you should have been a girl. A clever girl. You're a useless bastard with no spine. And now look at you, in that bra and those...knickers. And that doll. What the fuck...do you...think you—"

He hadn't allowed her to finish. Had pressed his hand to the top of her head and kept her submerged. She'd flailed. She'd splashed him until he'd been soaked, but she'd given in eventually and had gone still.

"That's enough thinking," he muttered now. He walked around the flat to check it was sufficiently pristine for when his new guest arrived. "Time I add a bit to my diary, have something to eat, then go off out."

He'd prove that Langham pig wrong.

# CHAPTER FIFTEEN

Langham stood behind a wide oak in the forest, Oliver by his side. Fairbrother was behind, a few feet away with Hastings for company. Langham had questioned that—the kid might fuck things up due to his inexperience—but Fairbrother had countered that the young officer had to learn some time and that Fairbrother would take responsibility if something went wrong. Langham had continued arguing, saying they couldn't *afford* for anything to go wrong, not with one of their own out there, vulnerable and ready to be picked up by some nutter, but Fairbrother had gone to the chief who had overridden Langham.

Villier had walked the perimeter of the field twice now, each rotation taking her twenty minutes. She didn't rush, just like Langham had told her, and had her head bent most of the time, hands in her pockets, feet looking massive in the size eight trainers she'd bought—the only ones she could find in her rush after visiting Cheryl in hospital, she'd said. Langham had sighed, telling her how wearing footwear three sizes too big might be a hindrance tonight if she had to run, and she'd shrugged, saying she had the dog as backup, and running wasn't something she planned on doing. Something she shouldn't have to do, seeing as other officers would be on scene. Despite her brave words, she'd blinked, looking at him with a mixture of apprehension and uncertainty in her eyes.

She whistled the dog. It came running, its long stride and body movements a sight of beauty. The German Shepherd—black and tan—reached her side, and she took one hand out of her pocket to give him a treat. Great bastard of a dog, it was, his back level with the middle of her thigh. Langham wondered if they'd done the right thing choosing that breed. A smaller dog might have fared better—less menacing, less of a warning to the killer that he might want to keep away—but they needed the Shepherd's strength in taking the man down.

Langham peered into the forest, just barely making out the buildings of the estate showing through the trees in the distance. Someone was parked down there, ready to tell them if anyone was on their way to the field from that direction. Langham didn't think he'd choose that route, though. He reckoned he'd park up and walk around, entering the field from the Morrisons side. A man emerging from a forest and approaching you was more threatening than one just appearing as though he was using the field to cut across on his way through the woods to the estate.

At least, that was Langham's take on it.

He pulled his gaze from Villier, making sure Fairbrother was watching her, then turned to Oliver. He was staring at the field as though terrified he'd miss something, miss seeing the killer being caught.

Langham gave the field his attention once more, Villier out of sight. She must have reached the far bottom corner again. The trees were too thick for him to see that far, the opening from the forest onto the field only a few metres wide, but Fairbrother and Hastings would be able to spot her. Langham glanced across and, with no expression of interest on either of the men's faces, he surmised Villier was just walking. Just throwing the ball for the dog.

"Time?" he whispered, chin tucked low so his voice carried into the hidden microphone beneath his jacket lapel.

"Nearing nine o'clock," a voice said in his earpiece.

Fuck. They'd have to pull Villier out soon. Another few rotations and she'd have been walking too long. They could manage up to seven laps at a stretch, but that was pushing their luck. Besides, would the killer even be out this late? Yes, it would be easier if the man had the cover of darkness, but he'd taken women last summer at an earlier time, when the sun hadn't yet set and other people had been about.

He had balls, this one.

Langham shrugged off a shiver and let out a long breath as Villier came into view. She seemed so different in those clothes, not the ice-queen bitch she was in uniform. She almost appeared...nice. Approachable. And that was what they wanted, what they needed, wasn't it? Just some woman taking her dog for a walk, with her boring, straight, long brown hair and blue eyes that had itched so much back at the station she'd said she'd wanted to rip the contacts out.

He continued staring, adrenaline kicking up. Continued waiting, heartbeat growing erratic.

Something had to give.

David stood in the far corner of the Morrisons car park. He'd left his Fiat a few streets away from his usual parking spot behind the forest—he'd got the funny feeling he'd had before—and while he'd walked to this spot, he'd had to think about how he'd handle tonight. Parking so far away, and in plain view of the estate's residents, too, meant he'd have to make friends with the woman, encourage her to go with him. The dog, as well, like he had with the Yorkshire Terrier slag. It was a bind, something he could do without, but that feeling in him had been strong. He'd told himself he was imagining being watched, that he'd got the jitters because he hadn't had a chance to plan this one. That was all it was. That was *all.*

He stared across the expanse of tarmac, over car roofs, past late-night shoppers pushing trolleys laden with goodies towards their cars. He fixed his sights on the field over the road, ignoring the people who intermittently bobbed about in his peripheral. They weren't important, weren't anything to worry about. Were they?

Of course they weren't.

Some woman had been walking her dog over there for a while now. Seemed like she was lost in thought, had troubles on her mind, staring at the ground like that. She'd be easy—and only her and her dog had occupied the field for the past hour. So why was he hesitating? Why didn't he just go over there and talk to her?

*What if she's like all the others? What if she ends up hating me once we're back at my place?* Doubt was a whore, spreading its legs and inviting him to take a closer look at its messy redness.

"What should I do, Mr Clever?" he asked.

*"I already told you, David. If you choose to ignore me, think about what you might have passed up. What if she's the one? What if she's here visiting family for the night and won't ever come back here to walk her dog again? What if you miss your chance?"*

To get away from Mr Clever, David strode across the car park and stepped onto the field, the grass springy underfoot, a vast difference to the concrete. A surge of belonging stole into him, like he was at home here, in the right place at the right time. His worries had all been for nothing. He could do this. He could switch on the charm and wrap this woman around his little finger.

He approached her as she headed towards the forest opening end, keeping his steps languid, hands in his fleece pockets, closing his fingers around the full syringe, just in case. If he had to, he'd drug her with enough shit that meant she'd stay asleep for hours.

She didn't glance up but continued walking. Her dog stopped running, halted, and stared across at him, ears pricked, tongue lolling out of the side of its mouth. It might be a big animal, but it appeared friendly enough. Didn't display bared teeth. Didn't have raised hackles. Didn't growl. Its eyes were keen yet soft. No, he wouldn't have a problem with this one.

"Hey, *nice* dog," he called, jogging until he came abreast of her.

She looked up slowly, as though coming out of a daze. "Oh, sorry. I was miles away." She smiled, then whistled. The dog trotted to her side. Stroking its back, she said, "Yes, lovely dog. Don't know what I'd do without him."

"Oh, I know what you mean." He gazed directly into her eyes.

They were bright blue. The brightest he'd ever seen.

*Christ, this is it. She's the one. I know it.*

"I used to have a dog once." He strode along with her. "D'you mind me walking with you for a bit, by the way?"

She shook her head and stared at the ground again. "Nope. Nice to have a bit of company. I don't get out much these days. Not since..."

What was up with her? She seemed upset. "Since...?"

"Since my husband died. That's why Jerry, my dog...why I don't know what I'd do without him. Companionship..."

David nodded, feigning understanding. "I'm sorry," he muttered. It was something she'd have expected him to say.

"Me, too, but being sorry won't bring him back. I need to move on, sort myself out. Who knows, there might be someone else waiting out there for me. I just want...I just want to love someone. Be loved back."

She lifted her head, stared right at him, and sincerity shone from her eyes.

*This is it, isn't it? She's so nice. But the dog will still have to go. I can keep the woman, though.*

"Listen," he said, coming to a stop at the forest entrance. "I know we've just met and all that, but do you fancy going for a drink? I mean, I realise it seems a bit weird, me asking you like this, but...well, you look like you could do with some company, and I certainly could. Been one hell of a day..."

She nodded, fast bobs of her head that jostled her hair, and smiled so wide the corners of her eyes creased. "I'd love to. That would be nice. Can Jerry come?"

"God, yes. I love dogs." *Liar.*

"Great! Do you want to go to the pub through there?" She nodded at the forest. "There's one on the edge of the estate. Nice place, and they don't have music in there. Be lovely and quiet so we can chat. I can chain Jerry outside to the railing fence."

David smiled. "Yeah, that'd be fine."

He wanted to laugh at how this was going. Everything was falling into place. He could get her to his car with no problem after he'd bought her a few glasses of wine and she was unsteady on her feet.

No problem at all.

Langham carefully stepped back, hoping to God his feet didn't dislodge something on the ground so it cracked. Time seemed to still, and the only sounds were the thump of his thundering heart and his majorly loud breathing. Villier and the suspect headed towards them, and Langham held the air in his lungs, almost closed his eyes because he couldn't bear to see if the man sensed them and everything went to shit.

Once Villier and her companion went past them, far enough ahead that movement wouldn't be heard, Langham guided Oliver to the other side of the tree. They watched. Villier chatted to the bloke, Jerry lolloping beside her, having been obedient in not sniffing at them or Fairbrother and Hastings when they'd walked through. They couldn't arrest the bloke yet—he hadn't done anything—but the pub scenario hadn't featured in their plans. Still, Langham knew where they were going and would follow, keeping out of sight as much as possible.

He spoke quietly into his mic, relaying the information to the officers just to be sure they'd heard the conversation between Villier and the man via their earbuds. After five minutes, Langham, Oliver, Fairbrother, and Hastings pursued, reaching the other side of the forest in short time. Before emerging out onto the street, Langham checked in to make sure he had the all clear. He got it as the four of them stepped out onto the estate path, then frowned, the idle chitchat in his ear turning to something more serious.

"Listen," the suspect said. "D'you mind if I go and get my car? It's parked just down here. I'd rather have it in the car park if we're going into the pub."

A knot of apprehension settled in Langham's gut, a painful ball. He glanced ahead at some red-brick houses—lights on, people at home—then down the street to the right where the unmarked police car sat—blue Ford Fiesta, the silhouettes of two officers inside.

"Okay," Villier said. "Want me to come with you?"

"Where are they?" Langham whispered into his mic.

"Go left," a voice said in his ear. "They're about two hundred metres along, right by the second unmarked car."

"Yeah, why not," the suspect said.

He sounded so normal, so genuine that Langham had the brief thought that he might not even be the one they were after. What if he wasn't? It didn't matter—officers were still positioned at Morrisons.

"Saves me sitting in the pub on my own," Villier said, her voice light. No traces of fear there. "Never was much good at that. Walking into a pub by myself, I mean. I'd rather have you with me. Saves any men getting the wrong idea, if you catch my drift."

Langham glanced at Fairbrother and jerked his head to the left. They split up—Fairbrother crossing the road with Hastings, Langham and Oliver staying on the right-hand side—and walked casually down the street. Just men on their way home from the boozer.

"Oh, yes, I know exactly what you're saying," the man said. "There it is. You see it? Just down there, look."

"Oh, yes. Nice little brown Fiat," Villier said.

*Jesus Christ, I wonder if it's him.* "Stand by," Langham muttered.

"Oh, how weird is that?" she said. "You have a number plate almost identical to mine, except where you have a three and an L, I have a six and an H."

She'd thought on her feet—they could run that plate and find out who he was.

"Really? Might be fate." The man laughed.

Langham didn't like the sound of his voice or that laugh. It was high-pitched—*like a woman*—and tinkled oddly. Sounded a tad manic if he were honest.

"Watch it," he murmured into his mic. "His voice has changed. He's on the turn."

"And fate *is* weird," David singsonged, wondering if she was being genuine, "but in a good way. Here we are. Let me just open the back door so Jerry can get in, then we'll be on our way." He shut the dog inside, then reached into his pocket for the syringe.

It felt good against his skin, something he could depend on. His voice had changed early—he didn't usually speak like that until The Time. It made him a little uneasy, and confusion bumbled around in his mind for a few seconds. He stared at her, silently questioning why she hadn't seemed to notice. She appeared the same—relaxed in his company, no signs of distress—and he told himself it was further confirmation that she was the right one for him.

That was good, wasn't it? Maybe this would be the last time he'd have to do this. Maybe he'd found the mother he should have had all along. Would she even want to act as a mother? She might want one of those *relationships* and expect him to fuck her.

Her expression suddenly changed, throwing him off-kilter again. She looked nervous now the dog was on the back seat, and glanced in at Jerry, one hand to her mouth, squeezing her bottom lip with her finger and thumb. He risked turning away to peer at the dog. It stared out at her, panting, his breath fogging the glass, nose pressed against it, creating a wet patch.

Just like he'd always thought. Smelly, dirty, disgusting animals. That wet patch would dry and leave a smeared grey mark. He'd have to clean it, lug his portable vacuum cleaner down all those stairs and get it to suck up the hairs that were undoubtedly scattered on the seat. And how the hell he'd get rid of that dog was anyone's guess.

He glanced at the woman again. "I just realised I didn't tell you my name." He stuck out his free hand, tightening the other around the syringe. "I'm Sally."

*Oh fuck. Oh, Jesus fuck, what have I said?*

The woman smiled, didn't seem fazed *at all*. What was up with that? Was she one of those types who accepted people for who they said they were? He knew somewhere in his increasingly foggy mind that she should have been surprised at the name he'd given. At least frowned before masking her surprise. Yet she hadn't. Something was wrong, wasn't it? Where was Mr Clever? Why wasn't he here?

"Nice to meet you, Sally," she said, smiling away. "I'm Cheryl."

*Another Cheryl?*

Panic whirred inside him. What was going on? Was this some kind of joke?

A babble of laughter erupted from him, and he let her hand go to open the passenger door. She stepped forward and placed one palm on top of it, resting her hip on the edge. He made a show of pretending he'd forgotten the seat had books all over it.

"God, let me just clear these off for you." He leant in front of her while frowning and wishing his voice would stop doing that. "Sorry about this. I read quite a bit. Just been to the library today. Good girl. Clever girl. Don't hurt me."

*Oh God. Why did I say that?*

As he swiped some books into the footwell with one shaking hand, he eased the syringe lid off with his other, fumbling because his fingers seemed to have thickened. Turning a bit, he spied her thigh to his left and pulled the syringe out, getting ready to lunge at her, to stab the needle into the muscles there beneath her baggy tracksuit bottoms.

"Get!" She clicked her finger and thumb then stepped back and took her hand off the door.

David wondered what the fuck she'd meant and frowned, readying himself for changing tack and waiting until she sat beside him before he jabbed her instead.

But Jerry bounded between the front seats and clamped his mouth around David's wrist, applying pressure and growling. David yelped, tugging his arm, panic ripping into him.

*Don't hurt me. Please, don't hurt me.*

The dog held firm. The syringe slipped from his grasp, and he stared at Jerry, at the spit dribbling from his lips, at how those big teeth indented his skin but hadn't pierced it. Something cold snapped around his free wrist, and he whirled from the beast to stare into the eyes of another woman, the eyes of someone who no longer had brunette hair but blonde.

Someone who looked just like the bogeywoman.

"I am arresting you on suspicion of murder…"

# CHAPTER SIXTEEN

Langham reached the Fiat and winked at Villier, letting her know that was a job well done. She acknowledged his praise with a nod of her own and smoothed down her real hair, flyaway tresses standing every which way. The wig was now a heap of synthetic fibres at her feet where she'd tossed it, one tress draped over the toe of her trainer, a furry tongue. He looked away from her, unable to stand seeing the relief mixed with fear in her eyes—she'd go into shock later, he'd bet, but for now she'd hold it together, if only so she didn't give anyone the satisfaction of seeing her crumble.

His dislike of her melted, changed into admiration. She might be a strange one, but she had guts, he'd give her that.

Langham gave the man his attention. One wrist was cuffed to the car door handle, the other clamped between the dog's teeth. He was bent forward, his back arched, head bowed, and his body bobbed as though he had trouble breathing.

Langham reached inside the vehicle and gripped the man's elbow while Villier took one end of the cuffs off the handle.

"Leave," Villier said.

The dog let go, sat on the driver's seat, and appeared to smile as though he knew he'd been good. Langham cuffed both wrists at the small of the man's back. He wrenched the suspect away and onto the path, into the hands of Fairbrother and a shit-scared-looking Hastings. They each grasped one of the suspect's upper arms, and Langham took a moment to study the killer who had taken so many lives.

Tears streamed down the man's face. He hiccoughed several times, odd noises coming out from between his overly pink lips. Was he wearing lipstick? He had the green eyes and blond hair Oliver had seen, although that hair wasn't a natural shade. It came from a bottle, no doubt

170

about it, and a home job, the strands of blond uneven. Langham tried to feel pity, tried to fathom what excuse he had for doing what he'd done, but found not a shred of it going spare.

"Take him away," he said, maintaining eye contact until Fairbrother and Hastings marched him down the path to a waiting, unmarked car.

"You all right?" He rested his hand on Villier's forearm.

She stepped forward, and he took his hand off, feeling she hadn't liked him touching her or showing compassion in front of any hidden officers watching. She clicked her finger and thumb, and Jerry gambolled out of the car then sat at her feet, gazing up and waiting. Villier huffed out an unsteady laugh, reaching into her pocket to produce a treat. She fed the dog, hunkering down, and wrapped her arms around its neck. Tears fell then, a couple of sobs erupting, and Langham had the grace to turn away, to give her time to process what she'd actually done—how things could have gone totally differently. She was shrouded by the car, no one else would see her meltdown, and he felt oddly glad about that. At one time he'd have wished she had witnesses.

Oliver stood staring at the pavement, hands in his jeans pockets.

Langham went up to him. "They'll be all right now he's been caught. Your mum and sister," he said.

Oliver glanced up, his eyebrows pulled together at the bridge of his nose. "I think I ought to go and visit them anyway. It's time to see if I can mend bridges."

With the Fiat towed away complete with evidence, and David Courtier's flat being searched for more, Langham just about had things sorted for now. Yes, there was a lot of paperwork to be done, a lot of interviewing, and many visits to the dead women's families to let them know their daughters' killer had been caught. It wouldn't bring the women back, wouldn't take away the heartache, but at least it would give them some measure of relief, closure.

He sat at his desk, his interview with David over, frustrated as hell because the man hadn't told him anything except that he was looking for someone to be his mum. The bloke had serious issues, was a fuckup, no getting away from it, and maybe a psychologist would fare better with him. David may or may not open up, but the evidence in the Fiat alone was enough for a conviction. Langham had had a call from Hastings, who'd opted to join those at the flat gathering evidence, to say they'd found a diary that Langham ought to read.

He was waiting on its arrival now, drinking coffee that tasted like gnat's piss—not that he'd ever tasted any to make that comparison—and munching on one of his biscuits. Oliver had gone home after the arrest.

Langham got up, stretched, the muscles in his back protesting, his bones doing the same with audible cracks that told him he was getting on a bit. Not that nearing forty was getting on, but it bloody well felt like he was older than he was at times. Like now, having had little sleep and wanting nothing more than his bed but knowing he couldn't have it for a few hours yet.

He left his office and went out into the car park for some fresh air. It woke him up a bit, shook the fog from his mind and invigorated his heavy limbs. It was daylight again on a Sunday morning that he should have sodding well been enjoying at home, lazing about in bed, knowing he didn't have to return to work until the following day. He didn't have another weekend off until a fortnight's time, but he'd sleep the sleep of the dead tonight, he knew that much.

*Not a good choice of words there.*

If he smoked, he'd enjoy several cigarettes before he went back inside to have another crack at Courtier. The man had been asleep in a cell the last time Langham had checked, and he envied him the oblivion. Did he sleep well? Who the fuck knew, but he dreamed, that much was certain. His eyelids had flickered, rapid movements, and Langham had walked away, shaking his head and wondering just what the fuck was going on inside that man's head.

David stood in his childhood living room again, facing the bogeywoman. She didn't look very pleased, as usual, and he watched her, wary, unsure of whether she'd spew her litany of abuse or get up and drag him into his room for a beating.

He wanted to shrug again—why did he always get the urge to do that when with her?—but resisted, clasping his hands behind his back, holding tight as though one hand belonged to someone else. Someone who gave a shit and had reached out to give him comfort. It was better than the truth, pretending like that, helping him in the calm before the possible storm.

She eyed him with that expression of hers, the one he feared the most. It meant she was about to do something horrible and he wouldn't be able to stop it. Meant he'd have to either leg it and hide or stand there and take whatever she dished out. That look had different degrees of scariness, and he'd learnt early on to gauge which one meant which thing. This one inspired all-out terror. He wouldn't be running and hiding. He didn't dare.

"You fucked up good and proper this time, didn't you?" she said, bouncing one leg over the other again. Her red high-heeled shoe came loose, dangling on her toes and flapping with her movement.

He waited for it to drop. Wondered why she always dressed as though she was going for a night out on the town. Dad had told David once that she'd worn normal clothes when he'd met her, casual things that made her just like everyone else, but when David had been born, she'd changed, hadn't she.

And it was his fault she'd become like she had.

His personal journey had come to an end, and he still didn't understand how the second Cheryl had been taken away from him like that. How the police had been right there as soon as that ugly dog had clamped on his arm. Mr Clever hadn't said a word since he'd encouraged David to approach Cheryl Mark Two in the field, and he felt lost without the guidance. Abandoned. Uncared for, again. That voice had been with him for so long that the absence of it felt alien.

"Where is Sally, David?" Mother asked.

David darted his gaze around the room, then released his wrist to check he didn't grip Sally's hand in his. The doll wasn't there. Reality further mixed with his dream world, and he knew the police would have his dolly now. She'd be frightened with strangers in the flat, unknown hands picking her up and inspecting her mangled face. And that reminded him of his mask, how, when he'd been taken into the police station, they'd asked him to empty his pockets and he'd laid it on the desk. The officers had glanced at one another, nodding, grim smiles stretching their faces into weird shapes, and one had said, "Fucking got him."

"Of course they got you, David. How could you have thought they wouldn't?" Mother asked. "It'll all come out now, about me, you'll see. Maybe they'll finally find what's left of me in that stream."

175

*Bones. Just bones.*

She rose, that look darkening, and David braced himself for the first impact of fist on cheekbone. Then the second, a fist in his stomach, fists every-fucking-where.

He crumpled to the carpet, letting her do her thing.

"Sally," he whispered. "I want Sally."

Oliver raised one hand then knocked on the door of his childhood home. Langham stood beside him on a large patio slab step, way beyond knackered, running on fumes. He didn't think it wise for Oliver to be here—he was inviting a shitload of hurt—but it was his choice and something Oliver had said he had to do. Not something Langham fancied himself on a Sunday afternoon, but there he was, being a good mate.

The blue door swung open, and a woman—Mrs Banks, Langham presumed—filled the doorway, her mouth dropping open. Her cheeks, bearing the ruddiness of a drinker, flared redder, and her eyes darted about, the woman clearly checking up and down the street. She had a red apron on over a patterned dress, dusted with flour and what appeared to be biscuit dough, making a mockery of what a mother was supposed to be like, as in reality, she was far from that.

Langham disliked her more already.

"What do *you* want?" She focused her attention on Oliver. "I told you when you left I didn't want to see your sorry arse again."

She reminded Langham of David's description of *his* mother—that diary had answered all his questions, and he'd almost, *almost* felt sorry for the man. To realise that David was the David who Conrad Leddings had mentioned as being the man he met for breakfast most mornings had come as a shock.

"I just..." Oliver shifted from foot to foot. "I just came to see if you were okay."

"Of course I'm okay, you weird bastard. Why wouldn't I be?" She narrowed her eyes and shifted her gaze from Oliver to Langham. "Look," she said, curling her top lip as she gave him the once-over, "you ought to sod off. I have neighbours who could see you." She stared at Oliver again. "Bad enough the pair of you are in the bloody paper, flaunting your weirdness for all to see, let alone being on my doorstep."

She was a bitch and half, this one, but Langham would let Oliver lead, would stand beside him as support until he decided it was time to go. In Langham's book that time was now, but Oliver didn't seem as though he planned on walking away yet.

"How's...?" Oliver began.

"Your sister? She's fine. Just fuck off, will you? Fuck the hell off!"

She stepped back then slammed the door.

Oliver let out a shuddering breath. "You told me so, yeah, I know." He turned. Brushed past Langham. Walked down the path to the car parked at the kerb. Waited at the passenger door.

Langham clicked his key fob, and Oliver got inside. Belted up. Langham was unsure whether to leave him be for a minute or two, or just join him and drive off, not saying a word. It was a difficult call.

He sighed and got in, starting the engine and peeling away. He wanted to tell Oliver that woman was the biggest cow he'd ever come across, that sometimes you encountered them in life and they amazed you with how nasty they could be. That she wasn't worth wasting time and energy over—emotions over.

"That told me, didn't it?" Oliver said, chuckling.

"It did."

"Jesus fuck, whatever made me think she'd changed?"

"Hope," Langham said. "It's strong in all of us. Even people like David Courtier. His diary...well, let's just say it would ring some bells for you."

"Takes people differently, though, doesn't it?" Oliver reached forward and popped open the glove box, taking out two cans of Coke Langham hadn't even been aware were there. He opened one and put it in the cup holder for Langham, then cracked the other and took a long sip. "I mean, we've probably had similar childhoods, and he's fucked up, I'm not. I don't think."

178

"You have your moments." Langham eased into a steady stream of traffic.

His phone trilled. He swore, several different words, their volume getting louder with each one. He wished that whoever was on the phone would end the call now so he wouldn't have to bother answering it. That someone else at the station had come along at just the right moment, giving him a reprieve. He contemplated letting it ring, saying when asked tomorrow that he hadn't heard it go off, that fuck, he must have been out for the bloody count. But he tossed the notion aside. He couldn't do it—didn't have it in him.

He pulled over and took his phone from his pocket. Surely it couldn't be Fairbrother. Surely the man could handle whatever had come in by himself.

"Langham. Right. Yep, I understand. If I come out, it'll just be to assess the scene for an hour or so, all right? I seriously need some sleep." He cut the call and turned to Oliver. "Got to go to work."

"I gathered." Oliver swiped the back of his hand across his brow. "Want company?"

"Not until—or unless—you can contribute. You know the rules. Only on the team if you're contacted."

"I hate that."

"That's the way it goes."

"What's happened?"

"Woman found battered. Well, two have, but it appears it's by the same person—same MO—so

179

while Fairbrother visits one scene, I get the other. Lucky me, eh?"

Printed in Great Britain
by Amazon